HOCKEY SUR GLACE

HOCKEY SUR GLACE

Stories

Peter LaSalle

BREAKAWAY BOOKS
NEW YORK CITY
1996

ISBN: 1-55821-505-0
Library of Congress Catalog Card Number: 96-85516

Published by:
BREAKAWAY BOOKS
P.O. Box 1109
Ansonia Station
New York, NY 10023
(212) 595-2216

BREAKAWAY BOOKS are distributed by:
Lyons & Burford, Publishers, 31 West 21st Street, NY, NY 10010.

Parts of this book have appeared, sometimes in different form, in the following publications: "Hockey Angels" in *Witness* and in the anthology *Sports in America,* edited by Peter Stine (Wayne State University Press, 1995); "Le Rocket Nègre" in *Boulevard;* "Goalies Are Weird" in *Interim;* "Wellesley College for Women, 1969" in *Kansas Quarterly;* "The Injury" in *Quarterly West;* "Hockey" in the collection *The Graves of Famous Writers,* by Peter LaSalle (University of Missouri Press, 1980).

For my godsons—Paul and, in memory, Michael

CONTENTS

ice hockey: a game played on an enclosed rink between two teams of six players wearing ice skates and using a thin-bladed stick to propel a hard rubber puck up and down the ice with the object to drive the puck past the opposing goalkeeper into the goal for a score and to prevent the other team from scoring.

—*Webster's Sports Dictionary*

It was not (to start again) what one had expected.

—T. S. Eliot, *The Four Quartets*

HOCKEY ANGELS

I was eleven years old in 1958, and I had a paper route. Our small mill city was deep in the woods of northern Rhode Island. In the thin sunlight of the December afternoons, everything—the red brick of the mills along the icy river, the buff-and-chocolate combo they inevitably painted the wooden three-deckers—took on the diluted softness of a watercolor. I used to read my way through the evening edition as I delivered, my unbuckled black rubber galoshes clanking, the rocky weight of the worn canvas sack on my shoulder lightening. Once on the city page there was a headline and a photograph.

MIRACULOUS MEDAL SAVES TEXTILEVILLE YOUTH

The accompanying story told how Eugene Ouellette of the Textileville neighborhood had fallen through the ice while playing choose-up hockey with a group of pals. They were skating at the mill-basin pond near the abandoned properties of the Leighton Lace Company. His friends managed to pull him out by making an

impromptu chain of themselves linked together by
their hockey sticks. The story told how the Textileville
"youth" later said to the reporter that he was never
scared in the course of the ordeal, where he sank maybe
clear to the leafy black muck at the bottom of the
frigid water and he was actually stuck beneath the ice
for a while. He probably pressed his palms against it,
his body surely twice its weight in the soaked winter
clothes. Yes, his friends eventually tugged him out,
and, yes, he had no fear at all, because he was wearing
an item commonly called a miraculous medal. He said
that as soon as the cold weather hit every November,
his mother gave him a new one to protect him on the
ice for the next several months, till the earth in the gardens smelled as rich as coffee grounds again and the
crocuses bloomed.

The photograph was grainy. It was of a decidedly
goofy-looking kid a little younger than me. He grinned
through crooked teeth. He wore a checkered wool jacket
and a knit toque pulled almost to his nose. And in one
hand he held up the miraculous medal, dangling it like
a minnow for the camera.

I knew what the medal was like. A small embossed
oval, cheaply plated gold, showed the robed Blessed
Virgin, her arms outstretched and stars all about her. It

hung from a baby-blue ribbon, in turn attached to a
pin, cheaply plated gold too. I also knew that a mother
pinning such a medal on her son's jacket was a ritual
that could happen only in Textileville, a neighborhood
once entirely owned by that lace company. Everybody
in our city by this point probably claimed some French
ties, even if you were from one of the original Yankee
families who founded the mills, or even if you were
from the sizable group of Latvians who came to work
the looms after the flow of the original Quebecois
down from Canada. But Textileville was Frencher than
French. It was poor as well, and in Textileville you
found shrines to St. Joseph in the worn backyards of
the tiny white rowhouses, and outdoor Stations of the
Cross, with lurid little oil paintings under glass depict-
ing each stop in Christ's suffering, there on the grounds
of the neighborhood church.

I remembered Eugene Ouellette from that picture.
His name stuck in my mind. Sometimes dreaming as a
kid I seemed to encounter him underwater. In that
greenness we were both fully dressed in soaked winter
clothes, and as I pushed hard against the underside of
the ice in a frantic mime, he just smiled the goofy grin
from the newspaper photo. He was wearing the miraculous medal on the checkered wool jacket, and he was

quite at peace. Call him my first hockey angel.

In my senior year of high school I got into a pre-dictable-enough mess. I was sure that my girlfriend Maryanne was pregnant. It was a situation that I could have been dreaming too, it felt so farfetched. I hadn't even taken a girl to a movie before I met her at one of the Mount St. Paul's Academy Friday-night "canteen" dances the previous year. And suddenly, there I was, thinking about marriage and some kind of a job, and no longer having the heart to look at the catalogues for Williams College in Massachusetts or Dartmouth in New Hampshire. The very scenes of the tweedy, crew-cut undergrads carrying their books along autumnal paths in between classes seemed another assault on any hope of possible happiness for me.

I had studied pretty hard at Mount St. Paul's, honors list all along. I even surprised myself by doing well on the SATs. I was liked by the other guys at the boys school enough to be elected either class treasurer or class vice-president every year. And my running track in the fall and spring would probably convince any admissions officer that I wasn't simply a grind. My uncle who raised me had only a clerk's job, but both colleges were sure that along with my acceptance letter in April—which both were entirely confident about—would be a scholarship offer. What made the situation worse was that I wasn't in love with Maryanne, and I knew she wasn't in love with me, though she went overboard with declarations of that now. Before meeting me she had been dating a guy a half-dozen years older. Maryanne's father was a man who supported the big family with his lifelong job at a tool-and-die shop that had located in one of the former mill buildings. So the ex-boyfriend having a lot of ready money to spend would understandably impress her. The ex-boyfriend sold insurance for his father's agency, drove a yellow Chevrolet Impala convertible that could turn heads in a city as small as ours. I knew Maryanne was still in love with him. I knew I could forget about college.

Somehow, this all eventually involved Brother John Connell there at Mount St. Paul's. He was my second hockey angel.

In that senior year a group of us from the disbanded Mount St. Paul's varsity hockey team made the long drive from the mill city to Providence to rent ice time. Late on Saturday nights we played hockey among ourselves in a rink near big warehouses that had once been part of a shipyard during World War II. It was 1965.

The hockey was all I had to look forward to then. We got the ice cheap from eleven till one in the morning, and there was always something very special to skating top speed around the fluorescent whiteness while others slept. Sometimes we convinced the rum-nosed old boozer who ran the place to play Beatles albums over the loud-speakers, and in that smell of refrigeration that could cut like wonderful ammonia as you breathed, the blades ripped, the sticks slammed, and the puck knocked off the scuffed boards with echoes like somebody hammering in the country. Lennon and McCartney came together for that rare Liverpool whine that was truly best on "Anna" and "Please Please Me."

That night, as usual lately, somebody had to stop at the brothers' house at the school to pick up Brother John Connell. A guy about thirty, he was teaching at Mount St. Paul's after a couple of hitches in the order's East Pakistan missions. He was forced to leave when the fighting turned dangerous. He somehow received permission from the headmaster, Brother Maurice, to join us for our midnight sessions. He had played a good deal of hockey in upstate New York, I think, and even now he still had his moves. He held his own out there with us teenage guys in his CCM Tacks that looked ready for the museum and an authentic Detroit Red Wings jersey he had picked up somewhere along the line. The three car-loads of us usually traveled in a convoy, which was the kind of thing that could be fun then. But seeing I had the duty of giving Brother John a ride that week, those packed in my car wouldn't join the little caravan of sorts.

Mount St. Paul's sat on a genuine hill. It was a dark sil-houette in the blue cold of that January night. I swerved into the parking lot on the lower campus, easing past the shut-down school rink and heading toward the fieldstone brothers' house. Brother John waited outside. He wore full pads and an old army parka opened to reveal the Red Wings jersey. He held his stick like a staff, had his equip-ment bag over his shoulder Santa Claus fashion. I ap-proached him—then tromped the accelerator to jet the Dodge past him, jamming on the brakes and jerkingly backing up. He half-jogged toward the car, and when I rolled down the window Brother John was smiling.

"Hey, how ya doing," I said. "Gordie Howe, right? Look, Gordie, we're looking for this guy, a brother at the school who's supposed to meet us out here. Brother John Connell."

"Funny," he said in his easy, good-natured way.

"Wow," I said, putting on. "Look, guys, it's him! Sorry, Brother John, I saw the Detroit uniform and I could have sworn you were Gordie Howe."

"Yeah, yeah, yeah. I should put this stuff in the trunk, right?"

I handed him the key. Bobby Cassady sat in the front seat with me. He slid over. He knew all along that I had it in for Brother John, for who knows what reason.

"That Gordie Howe joke was funny," Bobby said flatly, then paused. "Funny the first time you pulled it about a month ago."

Why did I have it in for Brother John? On one level I could say it was because the school had taken varsity hockey away from us. Brother Maurice, that new head-master, had a record for reorganizing some of the order's other financially shaky schools. Despite his name that echoed that of beatified Maurice Rocket Richard himself, he looked at the books and was soon convinced that a major drain of money came from keeping a hockey team outfitted, plus the expense of running the decrepit rink that had a troubled compressor about to cough its last. He didn't care that Mount St. Paul's had its long hockey tradition. The school still attracted day students from the whole pocket of the state. And after World War II, Mount St. Paul's in its feared red-blue-and-white uniforms tore up the Class A division of the Rhode Island schoolboy league, admittedly with the help of many nasal-accented ringers imported from Quebec. Though the teams hadn't been too strong lately, having slipped into Class B and a cellar contender in that class too. Still, wasn't it the ultimate irony: the school had taken away hockey, and now one of its brothers showed up on Saturday nights to pitch in his two bucks toward rental, as we had to drive the long forty-mile round trip to find a rink we could afford.

But, in truth, I had always liked Mount St. Paul's. Around the city even on weekends, I wore my shabby blue blazer, the "MSP" on the pocket in once-white embroidery now as dirty as old string. Without the problem I currently had, I would probably have agreed with Brother Maurice that a drain like varsity hockey, as much as we all loved it there, would sink the school in the end. And I would probably have been a good pal indeed of a guy like Brother John. He had his easy way. He showed obvious concern for my best, even showed pleasure in knowing that it appeared I would be getting the opportunity that most Mount St. Paul's boys never got, the chance to go to one of those topnotch colleges on a scholarship. Neither he, nor anybody else, knew that I had gotten a girl pregnant, and that she was the girl who still talked about how "cool" the continental wheel was on her ex-boyfriend's Impala. Brother John didn't know that at this time next year I would be working to support a kid and a boring wife who wasn't very interested in me to begin with. So I hated the way Brother John wore the white, rather than black, cassock-style habit around the school. It was supposedly a practice required of brothers who had put in missionary time, and it served as an advertisement for that branch of the order's work. And I hated the friendly way he joked with me in our American history class that he had taken over at midyear. And I hated most the way he could say to me, almost dreamily, as if he were wondering if his own life might have taken a different course, that "You've got the whole world waiting for you, Mark. You'll make something out of it. I know it, man."

On the ice that night, I made sure that when we split into two groups for teams that Brother John was on the opposition. I made sure that any chance I had to bang the guy I did. In my tallness I was more skinny than big. But Brother John with his crooked nose, short-cut hair, and perpetual smile was thirty, and any shot to somebody thirty from somebody eighteen would hurt. The Beatles played, the game raged. Once I saw him deep in his own corner. He was retrieving the puck, his goalie having routinely flipped it back there. There was nobody else with him, and I was alone too, maybe five yards away. It happened fast, but it was almost gummy slow motion—as I dug in my skate blades hard to accelerate, held one elbow up for the spear, and slammed him with everything I had. The boards were as solid as poured concrete, the glass above them harder. He could have been a fly splattered on the wall. Play kept going afterwards, but I could see that he was shaken when he returned to the bench to let somebody else take a turn on defense for him. I returned to ours, huffing.

Bobby Cassady was there. He looked at me, then shook his head.

"That was cute," he said. The sarcasm was overdone.

"What?" I pretended to be interested in the play on the ice.

"'What?' he says. What the hell is the matter with you is *what*. What's this full-time jerk award you're trying to go for lately is *what*." He left me there, going back to take his own turn on a line. Brother John joked with me about it later. We were unlacing our skates. He smiled and admitted that he had surely left himself wide open for that nailing. I didn't joke about it.

Afterwards, we all went to Mass at the Franciscan chapel in downtown Providence. They offered a service at two on Sunday mornings. With Mass out of the way, we could sleep as late as we wanted the next day at our homes, nicely sore from the banging. I used to savor that soreness. And it used to be great to doze right till noon —great *before* my problem, that is.

I had a plan. This was where I was really going to get Brother John, not on the ice. I would expose him. Because wasn't it funny, a little suspicious, that somebody who was a religious brother said he would just as well stay there in the car? He claimed he would have to go to Mass anyway in a few hours with the rest of the brothers at the school. The Franciscan chapel in Providence was new and in an alley off Weybosset Street. In essence this was a drunks' Mass, a lot of tipsy folk attending after the bars closed, and in essence on Saturday night that end of the city's downtown could be seamy. Drug dealers, prostitutes too, in those scarlet go-go boots and ever-so-small miniskirts they wore even when the temperature on a snow-crusted night like this wasn't much above zero. At Mass we still had on our pads and coats, and I motioned for the other guys to let me slip out of the pew right after the gospel. The chapel in the basement was packed. I headed up the stairs and into the cold, determined. In my, well, madness, I was convinced that I would find what Brother John of the lily-white cassocks and the ongoing understanding was all about, what he was *really* up to on these sleazy streets. A Hispanic girl leaned against a Checker Cab across the alley, eyeing me. She was younger than me and heavily made-up. She wore the standard go-go boots and a short jacket of fuzzy brown stuff that reminded me of a teddy bear. Who was Brother John trying to kid?

So I walked the streets a little crazy for a good fifteen minutes before I gave up. I finally went to the lot where the car was parked. I suppose I knew all along that I should have started there. I suppose that when it appeared from a distance that the car was empty, I had no doubt either that he was there, that he had been there all along. My desert boots squeaked on the packed white. I stepped up to the car.

Brother John was sleeping. He lay on his side on the back seat. He was almost in a fetal curl, wearing the army-surplus parka and the ridiculous Red Wings jersey. His stubble dark on his face, he nevertheless looked boyish, the way his hands and knees were tucked close to him. He was sleeping because it didn't, in fact, make any sense for a religious brother or anybody else to go to Mass twice when that exhausted. And what the *hell* had I been thinking? Yet just then I was maybe thinking nothing. The stars above me in the inky sky were huge enough to be matches flickering, and it was somehow so right to be staring through the glass at the man sleeping and sleeping like that. It was somehow so right to be that close to somebody, and also wondering where—all the millions and millions of miles away—he traveled in his peaceful dreams, that hockey angel.

I couldn't remember when I myself had last been as relaxed.

Eugene Ouellette. Brother John Connell. They were just two hockey angels. I live in Southern California now. All this honeyed sunlight, and streamlined shopping malls, and shrubs like agave and palmetto that might only have been names in a nature text if I hadn't ended up out here. But thinking about Rhode Island, I seem to suspect there were other hockey angels back very long ago in those winters. Maybe the urchins who I would see hanging around rinks when we played Bantam League games. Bantam League for me would have been in between the Eugene Ouellette story and the Brother John story. You know, those scruffy toughs who you still surely see, kids always pug-nosed and pinching cigarettes between their smug lips, who unlatch the gate for the Zamboni to come onto the ice, who use their big squeegees to smooth the layer of wet around the red goal pipes so it will freeze evenly, who shovel the snowy shavings that the growling robotic contraption sheds in clumps as it bangs back over the threshold hump and through the gate again. Those kids known as "rink rats," who can probably outskate and outstickhandle anybody their age, but in their wild delinquency—do they go to school? do they even have parents and homes?—would never submit to anything as square as organized team play. Maybe they live in the rinks like ghosts, haunt the high rafters when nobody else is around, know the peace there that Eugene Ouellette knew as he wore his miraculous medal and smiled so near to death, that Brother John Connell from the dangerous foreign missions knew as he slept like a heavenly whisper in the back seat of my uncle's dark-green Dodge Coronet sedan in the other world of 1965.

"Does any of this make any sense?" I ask my wife.

I have been talking to her in bed in the darkness, long after our three daughters are asleep. No, my wife isn't Maryanne from the mill city. As it turned out, Maryanne wasn't pregnant after all, and the scholarship to Williams, if not Dartmouth, did come through.

"What?" my wife whispers.

"What I've been telling you now," I say. "These stories. This business of hockey angels." She has listened to the whole thing.

"Shhh," she says.

"I'm happy," I say.

"I'm happy too," she says.

"Hockey angels," I say low, to myself.

"Now sleep," she says. "Just sleep."

And I will, dreaming.

LE ROCKET NÈGRE

Tommy O'Brien wasn't black, or true black, anyway. He was almond color. And he had green eyes, emerald. Those eyes maybe did trace back to his Irish father. In manner and demeanor, however, he was always French. He was Montreal French, though Tommy O'Brien was never to skate for the beloved Canadiens there.

Later, when Tommy became a lionized cause of sorts, the popular press in Montreal would like to say that his mother was a prostitute from Port-au-Prince. The usual story claimed she was so beautiful that the visiting British viceroys or earls who came to give still another speech on Commonwealth solidarity in Ottawa always stopped at least a night in Montreal, simply to sample her exquisiteness. That was in the 1930s. But, in truth, she was but a domestic in an Anglo financier's house in one of those posh neighborhoods built onto the slope of dark Mount Royal itself, and the only contact Tommy had with his sailor father was the legacy of that Irish name. His mother died quite young, probably of tuberculosis, and Tommy was taken in by the Brothers of Holy Ghost. It was a very French order (the translation gave proper stress to the "of" Holy Ghost—Saint-Esprit—which was the town in northern France where the order was founded), and the red-brick orphanage was in the neighborhood locally called Balustradeville, because of the little wood tenements with their frilled, iron-railed balconies. Balustradeville was a place of men in berets and blue smocks drinking liter bottles of hard cider in corner taverns, a place of the constant clamor of knocking sticks and a skidding puck in the streets, when the sky streaked those unheard-of shades of pastels that maybe you do only get in sunsets so far north.

For Tommy, one life went on inside the classrooms of the orphanage. The brothers had black robes shiny from wear, and they perpetually pointed to the chalking on the blackboards or to the dead maps of the faraway rest of the world hanging on the cracking yellow walls. The cast-iron radiators clanked, the big clocks ticked and ticked. The other life went on on the river.

Most years, the St. Lawrence was locked with ice by the middle of December. The boys who put in their long hours there never joined school or church teams. Yet they themselves seemed to know that, urchins or not, they were playing the best hockey of anybody their age in all of East Montreal—possibly in all of the city, where hockey was everything. If there were four games going on on the ice that was hard and black with the first freeze, before the real snow, the gradations weren't based on how old you were; it was a matter of how good you were. At first Tommy wasn't very good. Quite skinny for his age of ten, he got to play some with these toughs only because they were toughs, from the orphanage or, if they had families, from the slums. They liked the small triumph, even defiance, of having a Negro among them as a pal. Those were endless afternoons indeed of constant hard play: reddened faces, the rain of shouts of "Out here, I'm clear!" and simply "Pa-a-assss!" in their nasalized French. Old wool toques on their heads, old checkered wool jackets that got tossed once the boys were warm, scarves flying like streamers against the backdrop of the lumpy old city at the foot of the silhouetted mountain, atop which the light bulbs in the cross glowed as strong as stars by the time Tommy tramped back to the orphanage at five.

Who knows how the change happened. It could have been that at fourteen Tommy just filled out. He was lanky still, but strong. Or it could have been something much more simple. Because that fall when the cardboard box of donations came in for the brothers' annual charity drive, Tommy wasn't so easily pushed aside by the others in the scramble for the loot. He didn't have to settle for another pair of skates with rusted blades and leather worn limp, the kind sold in the bargain basement of some department store on St. Catherine Street to begin with. There in the vestibule, he fought his way past the big toothless thugs like Guy LaFlamme and Peppy Thibodeau. He came out with two things: a pair of skates that seemed new and close to his size too, and the clutching hand of Brother Réjean on the back of his neck. As Tommy grew bigger, the brothers became uneasy around him, despite his shyness; they responded physically. In any case, Brother Réjean would figure into what happened to Tommy later, and, in any case, the skates were well worth the scuffle. They weren't cheap department-store fare. They were genuine CCMs, probably donated from the large house of another Anglo in rich Montreal, such as the one where his mother had been a servant. Just trying them on while sitting on the edge of his bottom bunk that very night, Tommy knew they were a find. They fit snugly, the strong arch as high as the Jacques Cartier Bridge under him, or so it felt. The

leather was still glossed its brown-and-black combina-
tion, and staring at them more and more, Tommy
knew how they were going to cut and dig for him.

In his life, Tommy O'Brien would repeatedly have
this dream. It seemed that he was in a very hot country.
It seemed that it was true jungle, not anywhere in the
Caribbean, where his mother was from, but more likely
somewhere in that damp ongoing greenness of hanging
vines and leaves as big as draped banners; he was in
Africa. There was a village of yellow thatch huts, and in
the dream it was always dark night, while everybody
else slept. It seemed that Tommy was always coming
back from somewhere out there, far into the darkness,
that he had been looking for something, as the others in
those huts continued on deeper and deeper into dreams
of their own. But if Tommy happened to run into somebody when he returned—once it was a child, another
time it was an old man, white-haired and just bones and
skin, who told Tommy he couldn't sleep, hadn't slept in
years—yes, if Tommy happened to run into somebody,
it was as if Tommy knew where he had previously been,
knew what he had seen out there, but he didn't have
the words to tell anybody exactly what it was.

The parrots squawked, the monkeys jabbered, then

it was still. It was no use.

This is the way it was the afternoon that Tommy O'Brien was discovered.

It was the middle of winter, in February. And it had been cold enough that year that some freighters were frozen into the solid white ice, which must have been several feet thick. Tommy was fourteen, and he had those CCMs. With his newfound ability that simply left him very confident, Tommy played with the best of the skaters for the impromptu river games. The scenario was strange. A Mr. Forsythe, who represented shipping lines, happened to be down at the river to determine if it would be wiser to unload whatever was left of an ice-blocked ship's cargo and send it inland by truck, or wait for a hopefully early thaw, though thaws in Montreal often never came until May. The snow lay deep in the city now, and for their games the boys had months before shoveled away a rectangle on the surface, which was admittedly pretty chewed up by this time in the season. Tommy cut and wheeled, side-stepped with all the grace of a dancer, and scored a couple of times. The goal he was attacking had been made by using two buckle-up black galoshes to mark it. But not just out on the open ice, as on the other end;

behind this goal, as a backstop, rose the huge riveted
hull of the freighter, its red paint streaked with rust.
Maybe it was the loud clanking sound of another bullet
of a shot ricocheting off the metal that caught Forsythe's attention. He watched the play that went on so
far below the deck that it must have looked truly distant, and others later said that Forsythe's first reaction
was succinctly, inquisitively, "What the hell?" But if the
response was to Tommy's ability or to the shock of seeing a black hockey player was never clear. What was
evident was that Forsythe, in his black fedora and over-
coat, watched Tommy, and he didn't take long to begin
his negotiating—if that was the word—with Brother
Réjean back at the orphanage. Brother Réjean was the
superior now, the equivalent of headmaster, and his
manhandling of Tommy had gotten no lighter. In fact,
Tommy told him outright that he didn't like the plan,
even if this Mr. Forsythe had made a hefty contribution
to the orphanage as a token of his good faith in general
and his concern for Tommy's future in particular.
Tommy told Brother Réjean he didn't want to leave his
friends, and he especially didn't want to leave Montreal
and head to the boys school in Rhode Island, what
Forsythe had already arranged. The big brother landed
a real clout of his meaty hand on the side of Tommy's

head, as if to knock some sense into him. Tommy was too old for that now—he sprang at Brother Réjean and sent him clattering over a few rows of oaken desks there in the empty classroom that afternoon. Tommy would remember the snow falling and falling outside, almost hypnotically, and below in the street a growling orange snowplow snored by, its chains clanking. And Tommy would remember how Brother Réjean next got up and wholeheartedly thrashed him, for Tommy was only fourteen and no match for the man. Tommy later wished he hadn't done it; he knew that Brother Réjean, looming bully that he could be in his swaying robe and frayed Roman collar, was rather pathetic and was often heard by the boys crying alone in the cubicle of his room at night.

Forsythe always kept an eye out for talent for Mount St. Paul's Academy. It was located in a mill town in the hilly New England woods toward the northern border of Rhode Island.

As it turned out, the uprooting of Tommy wasn't as bad as he had feared. Mount St. Paul's served boys from French families in the area. Yet the hockey team was almost entirely composed of ringers imported from Quebec Province—not necessarily from the city, as with Tommy, but usually the country and the failing dairy farms in those forgotten towns that always had an oversize red-roofed stone church more fit for the Loire Valley than anywhere in the supposed New World. Mount St. Paul's was the perennial Rhode Island schoolboy-league champion, and it was appealing to Tommy that the school provided its own new rink for the hours and hours of drills and scrimmage; he also liked the look of the uniforms themselves. They were still genuine wool sweaters back then, not nylon yet at that stage right after World War II, with sewn-on satin markings; and they were direct imitations of the Montreal Canadiens' gear—the famous red-blue-and-white tricolor. If Tommy's own color was to cause problems, that was soon overshadowed by just how hard he played to show everybody his ability. He tied the school's goals record by his third year, and he took the state scoring title for that season as well. His speed was impressive. It was something first marveled at when he played in the New England semifinals in the three-tiered cavern of ancient Boston Garden. As Tommy worked on his line, he was noticing how he could surely feel the rumble of the steam locomotives easing into North Station below. The scant gathering of the press that covered the game was noticing that given this huge expanse of eerily white ice, much big-

ger than the rinks Tommy had banged around in for
schoolboy play in Rhode Island, this Negro kid had
time to accelerate and build up momentum, sometimes
untouchable when he eventually broke past the blue
line into the attack zone. Mount St. Paul's was elimi-
nated. But a Junior "A" scout from Montreal brought
back the word. Tommy had known from the beginning
that as strong as Mount St. Paul's was (there was a row
of brown-and-white photographs of championship
squads in the foyer of the school's rink), the caliber of
play was still American. It was definitely not up to the
level of Junior "A" where Peppy Thibodeau from
Tommy's orphanage days was now a defenseman. But
this scout was impressed, and when his reports
appeared as a squib in one of the French-language
sports sheets, Forsythe was heard from again. Actually,
he had been around all along, occasionally showing up
for a game at Mount St. Paul's when he was nearby, in
Providence on business.

"Tommy O'Brien is one of the last great river
skaters, I tell you," Forsythe loudly proclaimed. "In
five, ten years, when all boys are raised skating on
rinks, you'll never have a river skater again, somebody
who grew up playing in that wide-openness, a player
with his kind of speed, his kind of sheer movement."

Other hockey sheets maybe got carried away with Tommy's prowess, the notices fueled by Forsythe's direct attention now. They emphasized that Tommy was Negro. Typical was the story told energetically by Forsythe about the first time he saw Tommy play on the St. Lawrence. In the version that ran in one paper, Forsythe swore that when Tommy slammed a hard whip shot past the goalie that steely afternoon, it *poked a dent* in the hull of the ship from which Forsythe watched. Amazed.

Tommy was grateful to Mr. Forsythe for handling the agreement that sent him to Mount St. Paul's. But he discovered only later that he wasn't there at the school on an athletic scholarship at all. The Detroit Red Wings were quietly paying for it, just as they might be known to support an entire local or Junior team, if the boy they were backing was playing on it. Tommy suspected that from the start, anyway, and he suspected that Forsythe got his generous cut. Room and board, plus tuition, for most of the Quebecois there with Tommy at Mount St. Paul's were shelled out by different teams in the big league.

During the fifties Tommy skated in the American Hockey League, and his real problems began. For Tommy the biggest problem would always be that this wasn't a clear road back to Montreal, and Montreal was his home, where he wanted to be. For other people the problems with Tommy O'Brien were different.

Before expansion of the National Hockey League, the second-level American Hockey League offered competition of a high order. Some of the players shuttled in and out of the NHL, which was a very select operation with only a scant six teams then. Detroit, from the NHL, kept their option on Tommy, sending him to the Rochester AHL team. Suddenly race wasn't something that was merely stressed for accuracy, as in the hockey sheets in Montreal; it became an issue. If football long before had had its college black All-Americans, and baseball by this time had grudgingly opened up to blacks, with hockey the situation was more complicated. There had *never* been a black in all of professional hockey, and there was a strangeness to the entire idea of it that appeared to frighten some people, seeing that hockey was a game of the cold blue North, something unnatural to begin with for anybody of tropical descent. Tommy skated hard for Rochester, and he felt strong and fast, except on the team's road trips. There was some jeering, actually a lot of it in two cities in particular. Rochester had developed a keen rivalry with the team in Hershey, Pennsylvania, and the games there were always expected to be rough. The Hershey team was composed of muscle-bound bruisers who looked like they had shown up for a weight-lifting convention rather than a hockey match, and in their chocolate-and-silver uniforms, the very colors of the city's main product, they keyed on the young Tommy. It was close to a prize fight for him every time, the crowd sarcastically launching into their chant after a good crush; it was a takeoff on a current advertising line:

THE ONLY CHOCOLATE IS . . . HERSHEY'S CHOCOLATE

Tommy came to dread getting on the big-fendered bus for Hershey in his first year. Worse was leaving Hershey, inevitably cut up and aching with bruises.

In his second year the city was Providence, Rhode Island. It was all quite touchy. When Tommy had skated for Mount St. Paul's in that northern Rhode Island town, he was a local hero, even if he couldn't speak English very well and had been recruited from Canada. Now, when the Rochester team went to visit the Providence AHL team, Tommy was seen as a traitor. Plus, the hard-core working-class fans, who would pack a place like the Providence Arena to watch hockey, didn't have the simple niceties of the high-school crowds. Food was thrown at him. He might find himself in the corner wrestling with the opposition for the puck, and he might come out of the fracas bleeding profusely. Not from the on-the-ice banging, but from the work of whatever handy implement was shoved through the ragged chicken-coop wire atop the boards—no glass in such a decrepit operation— by a spectator. He was called "nigger" and "coon." And the locals started talking about Tommy's own guttural grunting when he kicked and elbowed the opposition in the continuous combat of another heated game. "Osti!" he would growl, "Tabarnac!" Or any of the other favorite terms in the cursing that was part of any French Canadian hockey player's vocabulary from about age six onward. (There lurked an element deep in the anger of the old peasantry of the region that made a verbal venting of it a matter of blasphemy, daring to shout the name of the holiest of objects, like "Host!" or "Tabernacle!") Somebody in Providence now translated at last what the fans had certainly been hearing from others for years without caring. Yet on the lips of Tommy, as handsome in his rage as any Othello, it became something else, and there were whisperings of Tommy being a literal "Black Devil" from some of the more crazed Roman Catholic overhearers, who went to their local parish priests in Providence for a reading on the whole thing.

Tommy made it through the first couple of years with the Rochester club possibly because he knew that in

the summers he could return to Montreal. He wasn't
one to socialize much with anybody during the season,
but in the summers he was known in Montreal; it meant
considerable celebrity status to be the sole black in pro
hockey. He was also one of the best players in the AHL.
Granted he wasn't up there with the league's ten top
scorers, but anybody who knew hockey had to admit
that it was amazing in itself for him to put in as much
time as he did on his shifts, having to face the rough coverage that he did. In Montreal in the summers he took
rooms in a hotel called The LaSalle, along with the old
orphanage friend, Peppy Thibodeau. Peppy now played
as a reserve on defense for Boston, a big-league city.
There was drinking in the clubs. There were girls.

To most outsiders, Montreal was just another out-
post in the winter—plenty of absurd cold and not
much more than that. But in the *summer.* It was the
fifties, and in the warm months Montreal was truly
what everybody often suspected it was: as close as you
could get to Paris without having to go there. The
evenings were balmy, leafily green. At the sidewalk
restaurants all over downtown, there were tables with
cloths so crisp you could still see the folds, maybe a
cut-glass vase of fresh purple or yellow gladiolus on
every one; white-jacketed waiters strutted with impec-

cable posture, beautiful young women sat with their handsome escorts, laughing lightly at something said in that whispery French in between sips of such excellent wine. Later on at the clubs, there was dancing, full bands featuring smooth lead singers in sequin dresses alluringly intoning more of that French, as the muted horns and throaty saxophones softly backed them up, and the dancing and dancing and dancing went on.

One night Peppy and Tommy had dates lined up with two sisters. The honey-haired girls worked as models for the same chic dress shop on Crescent. Peppy had met them, arranged for it all, and to Tommy he announced beforehand his claim to the younger of the two, a beauty with doe eyes named Renée. But there was a bit of confusion right from the beginning, and, as it turned out, this Renée had agreed to the date in the first place—she now confessed—only because she would be paired with Tommy. Peppy was irked, but good-natured about it. He wanted to get to the bottom of the deal, however, once he had had too much to drink. The girls giggled, joked about it themselves. Peppy reminded Renée that he played for the Boston Bruins, and he reminded her too that he had a new melon-and-cream Pontiac convertible. Renée wore a black sheath and long white gloves. At eighteen she showed a rare elegance; she had ivory skin, mile-high cheekbones, and lush lips like ripe fruit. But the elegance was totally lost in her reply to Peppy, another burst of prettily buck-toothed girlishness in her French:

"But he's Tommy O'Brien!"

"I see your point," Peppy conceded.

Tommy continued to pay what he saw as his dues. He stuck it out with Rochester in the winters, at least knowing he could return to the easy dream of Montreal for the warm months. The years passed, and there were more women in Montreal, and for a while, in the bruised summer evenings Tommy O'Brien could be seen on those streets lined with sycamores, wearing a cape and carrying a pearl-handled cane, possibly a girl on each arm and kids trailing after him and asking for his autograph. His flared nostrils, his chiseled jaw; he looked larger than life, though he was only five-nine or so.

Tommy was in his prime, and even if he wasn't playing for Montreal, he told himself that by now he should certainly be delivered from Rochester and brought up by Detroit. He won outright the AHL scoring title one year, goals and assists. Meanwhile, Forsythe, his self-appointed manager, continued to tell anybody who would listen that it was madness. The Canadiens had taken the Stanley Cup again, despite considerable concern over an injured Rocket Richard. Richard was more than important in the city; a couple of seasons earlier there had been gas bombs in the Forum and then public rioting in the streets when he was suspended from the play-offs for fighting. Forsythe was saying the almost outrageous: Why worry about the future of Rocket Richard and peg all hope for the Canadiens on him, when he was well past his prime, anyway; why didn't Montreal—the team, the entire city—come to its senses and do the necessary negotiating to acquire the rights to another one of their own, the player he called "Le Rocket Nègre," Tommy O'Brien? It was time they gave a Negro a fair chance in the game, forgot any quiet prejudices. It was time to break ground and not be content just to admire Tommy O'Brien from a distance, but to take a stand and finally bring him home, where he belonged. Tommy O'Brien was the real thing.

It became a set speech for Forsythe, who had played such a large role in Tommy O'Brien's life. The other man who had done that, Brother Réjean, had simply died. Tommy was getting older.

In that dream Tommy O'Brien was always coming back to the village of yellow thatch huts. He had known where he had been, but, again, he didn't have the words to tell anybody exactly what he had seen.

Tommy O'Brien finished out his career, pretty much forgotten, playing for a team on a level well below that of the American Hockey League, the Provincetown Peas. This was out on the tip of Cape Cod. (That the Montreal Canadiens had been willing—even wanted eagerly—to have Tommy O'Brien skate for them in the hallowed Forum no matter what his color, turned out to be a fact known only to a few people. And none of them would ever say much about it. If Tommy O'Brien's ability, without Forsythe's exaggerations, was affected at all by his color, it was because that color brought out a determination extra in him, as he tried to prove himself as a schoolboy player, and then in the AHL. But the couple of times he was actually invited to skate in the Canadiens' camp in September—quietly, close to secretly, via an agreement with Detroit—he crumpled. He was far out of his league there, no added effort could help that.) Playing for the Peas probably didn't offer competition much better than that at Mount St. Paul's, especially in those days right after the war, when Tommy had been part of that high-school team and when it stocked the solid prospects from Canada.

The Peas were part of an entity called the Lower
New England League, and most of the teams weren't
even farms for anybody. Though only a scattering of
people came to watch in any of the half-dozen small
towns in the system, it was worse at a summer resort
like Provincetown, which by definition couldn't supply
much of a population of locals to draw on in the winter.
The league was basically a depository for kids cut from
the real minor-league clubs, and they usually worked
days and got paid for hockey by the game; a few genuine once-pros, like Tommy, formed a core, earning a
more or less regular salary for the season.

So, in the midsixties Tommy put in his time as a
right wing in Provincetown. It could have been the
most unlikely spot imaginable to play hockey. The
ramshackle rink was close enough to the sea that you
could hear the foghorns and smell the saltiness. You
built up a sweat only well into the second period in the
drafty place, which sat on dunes with their dead yellow
sea grass blown in giant undulations under the big, big
ocean stars outside. More than once, in the middle of an
official game, an announcement came over the address
system for all able-bodied males among the hundred or
so assembled, spectators and players, to hurry down to
one of the town's wharves and man any available dories

and help in the rescue of a ship that was foundering in high swells out beyond the lighthouse.

The team existed in the first place only to satisfy the whim of an eccentric old textile-industry magnate. He had taken to living year round in his summer place there in the 1930s, and he started the Peas more as personal entertainment than anything else; the man loved hockey. One of his daughters stayed in Provincetown after he died, and she kept the team going maybe as a tax write-off or maybe out of her own eccentric homage to her father. She was middle-aged now, once privileged to that special world of ritzy private women's schools and exclusive horse shows, the latter her principal real interest back then, it seemed, considering that she had never married. Tommy moved in with the spinster.

She was often ill and confined to her bed. Tommy played his several games a week. He traveled in a battered station wagon, not even a bus, with some of the other players, to the various venues in said Lower New England.

Her house, where they lived, was a wood-shingle, single-story place, spacious. It was out on a point. In the mornings, Tommy often found himself alone in the big kitchen. If Tommy had had too much to drink the night before, after another one of those meaningless

Peas games that were becoming tougher to face, he sat, his head aching, at the table and sipped coffee and smoked cigarettes in the bright winter light. A row of tall windows formed one wall of the kitchen, and the view looked right over the stubble of brownish bare brush sticking up through the crusted snow, out to the massive wedgwood ocean beyond. The kitchen had a floor of black-and-ivory tiles, the light fixtures above were fluorescent rings. And Tommy could log hours there, staring at what always seemed to affect him most—the whiteness of the long line of enameled metal appliances and enameled metal cabinets. There was the lump of the streamlined stove, then the pillar of the streamlined refrigerator, then the lump of the stream-lined dishwasher beside that. Chrome trim and chrome handles, and, yes, that whiteness. But not just white—whiter than white with a capital "W." Or the white of thousands, no, surely millions, of square miles of the Arctic where nobody ever has, or ever will, set foot; the white of all the unpainted canvases dreamt by all the painters who are, or who were, or who ever will be. . . .

"The white," Tommy frequently murmured in his near trance. "The white, I tell you."

Some nights Tommy just drank, sleepless and raging at the sick woman about how she was no different than any of the rest of them, the pigs of those white fans in Hershey, Pennsylvania, or the pigs of those white fans in Providence, Rhode Island. Pigs like Brother Réjean and Forsythe, those who merely wanted to use Tommy for their own gain. It was his color, he told himself, that kept him from playing for the Montreal Canadiens. He had done what they wanted, and in the end he had deserved much more than what he had been dealt.

"I'm Tommy O'Brien!" he shouted at her in the darkness.

"Please," the woman tried to calm him.

"You'll listen to me. Somebody will listen to me. I'm Tommy O'Brien, and they had no right!"

Lately there have been reports that Tommy O'Brien, the legendary Rocket Nègre, has been sighted, found after so many years. Some of the encounters were easily refuted. In Quebec City, up in the far reaches of the province, it appeared that for a while every elderly black man who was seen washing crockery plates in one of those usual *hot dog steamé* cubbyholes with knotty-pine walls and green Naugahyde booths was rumored to be Tommy O'Brien. It turned quite bad for one aging, arthritic party who wanted only to be left alone, and he had to have his scripted birth certificate and a

photostat of his voter-registration card from the turbu-
lent sixties in Mississippi sent up by a granddaughter;
she tracked down the necessary proof in a county court-
house there that he wasn't Tommy O'Brien. And despite
such documentation to the contrary, word still lingered
that he was.

Somebody claimed he was living in Rochester again,
somebody else said they had spotted him in a town
near Hartford, Connecticut, home of a new expansion
NHL club. (There were other, quite crazed, reports.
Claims for a while that Tommy O'Brien had never even
played professional hockey, that there was only the *idea*
of Tommy O'Brien, the confused dreaminess in each of
us that shows us that life is just a wanting of something
we will never be, finding the big excuse for our failure
over and over, somewhere between the sadness of being
born and the darkness of being forgotten, which is
what dying is really about, anyway.) All kinds of stories
concerning Tommy O'Brien.

But a reporter's account about going to look for
Tommy O'Brien was somewhat different. A writer for
La Presse of Montreal, he was returning from a tour in
the Middle East, taking a few-day stopover in Paris. He
was named Pierre LaRocque, and he had no real desire
to return to Canada right away, to churn out a six-part

analysis series on the current wave of more confused terrorism in those countries. So he stayed on for a while in Paris. He drank cognac at the famous bar where Hemingway once drank, the one near the full wedding-cake grandeur of the Place de l'Opéra. And before long he did admit to himself that he finally was growing tired of listening to still another American journalist at the bar drunkenly rave about Hemingway's prose; or watching still another American tourist, inevitably in a newly purchased beret, ask one of the grouchy barboys to leave the coziness of low light on the varnish and brass in there, to step out to the fall dampness and snap a shot of him standing beside the entrance— where, of course, Hemingway had entered so often. And then LaRocque heard an accent entirely nasal and archaic; it had to be from a Quebecois. And then LaRocque found himself listening to a little man with a puppet nose say that in truth he didn't see anything special about Paris. He said he would just as well be back in his Montreal neighborhood of Notre-Dame-de-Grâce, and he said that if anything was to be gained from this trip it was his having run into Tommy O'Brien, who probably nobody remembered.

"Le Rocket Nègre?" LaRocque asked, suddenly interested.

"Somebody does remember," the man answered. "It was all by chance."

That afternoon, the reporter followed the directions that the little fellow had given him. To the Left Bank, up Rue Monge, and then farther up to Rue Broca and a narrow lane of cobblestones that shone like turtle shells in the easy rain. To a small, red-fronted *épicerie,* where the proprietor, a stooping old man of maybe an almond color, was completely rambling whenever the talk involved anything more complicated than asking for a green apple from the pyramid of them outside, or a larger box of wooden matches fetched from behind the counter. LaRocque soon concluded that this was but another example of another French Canadian (the little fellow in the bar) mistaking another elderly black (this tired proprietor in his gray jacket) for somebody who had once been very important to all of them. If there was a trace of a Quebec accent in this old man's French, LaRocque didn't detect it, so it was either never there or long gone. Whenever LaRocque did attempt to turn the conversation to hockey, the old man, now smiling, chose to ramble even more, not on that subject, but going on and on with some incomprehensible story about how he returned from wandering outside a village in Africa one dark night to try to tell the people there that he had seen something, something he couldn't quite explain to them. LaRocque was weary. He wanted to be out of the shop, and he knew it was time to face the failure of his own life (he should have stuck to struggling to write a novel when he had been young, not sold out to journalism), time to board a plane and return to Montreal; there he would have to write the so-called news he had no real interest in writing. Yet there was no stopping the old man and his talk. LaRocque, defeated, finally proceeded to walk away, and he never stayed long enough to hear the rest of what the proprietor had to say.

The old man continued to mumble to himself what he had attempted to tell LaRocque about. There in a dream of Africa, back from the shadowy jungle, he was in a village of yellow thatch huts, and at *last* he knew what was the something special he had seen, the enormous glassy expanse of it.

He paused, taken aback as he spoke it to himself now, aloud, smiling:

"Ice! Wonderful ice!"

SOME POEMS

A POND-HOCKEY PLEDGE

I will never do anything stupid
Like show off now in early middle age
With my old "moves" in what are these
Happy games involving wives and children.

I will never do anything *really* stupid
Like even challenge a twenty-year-old guy
Who earlier seemed to be saying something
To a pal about playing on the Bowdoin J.V.

I will wear my old CCMs, and the ragged
Red-blue-and-white Canadiens sweater no matter
How "dorky" my daughter says it looks; I will
Chase a lost pass, way, way down the ice.

When the others are gone I will skate
For a while on my own, blades ripping,
Muscles nicely aching, as the heartbreaking
Glow starts to show above the black fringe
    Of winter-bare trees.

GOALIES ARE WEIRD

I learned it early and firsthand:
In Bantam League in Rhode Island,
And Cal Hampton tended net for the wobbling
Bunch of us in genuinely moth-eaten
Green-and-yellow uniforms for the team
Sponsored by a local liquor store;
He swore blasphemously at opponents,
Said next to nothing to us,
Later became a Dominican missionary.

And on the intramural squad at college—
As far as I ever got—there was a loner
Behind the mask for us who listened to
Classical music, soft Brahms or softer Chopin,
To prepare himself for every game,
And then in the late sixties held the distinction
One apple-blossoming April day of being
The very first person arrested
In the City of Cambridge on
The charge of public LSD intoxication,
When he raced out of his rooms in Winthrop House
Wearing only Brooks boxer shorts,
To gracefully swan-dive into the blue Charles—

Two feet deep and filthy there.

Maybe I knew it all along,
And even before organized play
I had read how the famous "Wall" for
The Detroit Red Wings could never sleep
In the same hotel as his teammates on road trips,
For fear of his nightmares—
Trudging through orange flames? Afloat in
A lost skiff by moonlight?—infecting
The entire team, poisoning them to pure paralysis.

"Goalies are weird," I sometimes find myself
Whispering to myself, sensing I am
On the edge of realizing something *very* big . . .
Though I never know quite what.

HOCKEY SUR GLACE

This is what I want to tell you, dearest:
That maybe there is a home for
Old hockey players up by the golden angel
Of the Place de la Bastille
In the forgotten Twelfth Arrondissement
(I can't reveal the address);
That sometimes in the rain, after you
Have hurt me again, I maybe walk around
Right along the green Seine,
Under the graceful stone arches,
And I see an old man from there who was once
A deft forward for the Hershey, Pa., Bears;
Or in that favorite café on Rue Mouffetard
Where Arabs in black leather jackets
Drink and jabber, I see another one alone,
Wrinkled so under his tilted beret,
Who actually did make it to the NHL with Chicago.
The winter day goes sootily dark too early
In December now, and the wind down the cobbles,
Like my love for you, can slice to the barest bone;
But we are still young enough,
We can try again. And sometimes
I will edge right up to one of them

And whisper like a prayer, "Hockey sur glace,"
And he will nod just to get rid of me,
Dismissing me as crazy indeed,
As even he does not know how
I will return to you, love you still more.
Just listen to me, even if it makes no sense,
Repeat the singing syllables,
Feel how they surely can heal:

    "Hockey sur glace!" my dearest!

ROLLERBLADING ALONG

It's strange the way they rumble
When the asphalt turns rough, and
Though you sometimes think
In July's yellow heat (humid)
That you really *are* skating,
You can't help but look down to see
Your feet in the giant black-plastic pods,
Now pushing hard and harder
Up a gentle rise in a suburban street,
As you remember that all ponds are level;
Plus herein lies one of
The few ultimate truths to believe in life—
Most of the time, sad to say, *something*
Is at least better than *nothing*.

Wellesley College for Women, 1969

I got out to Alice's dormitory at about noon. I had driven the white heap of a Plymouth Valiant the fourteen miles or so from Cambridge on the local roads through Watertown, Newton, and the rest, rather than take the Turnpike. The traffic was never bad on Sundays once all the churches let out for the day.

I parked in front of the pseudo-Gothic mass called Haven Court in the January gray. I revved the engine a couple of times and listened to it sputter some more, even backfire in a loud rifle shot. I turned it off. Through the rearview mirror I watched as a cloud of smoke the color of pigeon feathers lifted in a single piece up above the black scribble of trees. My father (long a widower; he and I were more like a couple of buddies than anything else) had raised me on his own in the Maine city, and he had sold me the car the summer before for a token fifty dollars when he bought another. I think he would have given it to me outright. But we both knew I was beginning to get touchy around his generosity, especially when it came to my being at Harvard. Maybe that generosity had started the very day he drove me there to enroll a few years earlier, during Freshman Week. We lugged up the suitcases and the duffel bags, and he stood in the bare dormitory room looking out at the crisscrossing walks of the Yard, then down at a slate window ledge where so many initials had been carved by so many residents from so many years before: B. L. '99; W. de B. P. '05; J. P. O. '87, and such. He read them out loud. He pushed his olive porkpie hat back on his head, the crew cut that had often been white before it turned white because of his baker's job at the flour-dusty Tip Top bread factory. He stared and spoke low, more to himself than to me, maybe: "The famous men, the famous men who must have lived here. Go to all the lectures, Willy. Read all the books and meet all the famous professors. And remember, no working on the side for you, no crummy buck-and-a-quarter an hour. If that scholarship money isn't enough, then you just tell your broken-down old man, Al. I'll moonlight, I'll pump gas at Rousseau's Sunoco like I used to, before you miss out on one minute, on anything, these four years have to offer, kid."

I now patted flat a strip of red plastic tape I had used to patch the upholstery, an act done out of habit rather than any hope of success. In this kind of cold the stuff never had a chance of keeping stuck; it would continue peeling away corkscrew style like this till probably June. June, and graduation, being something I didn't particularly want to think about right then.

I lifted my gym bag with the skates and the battered hockey gloves from the trunk, and then the two hockey sticks.

I was surprised to see rolling around in there a can of Sunoco-brand dry gas. Sure enough, it had been left for me by my father, and obviously bought from Rousseau's station, for that matter, who knows when. Well, it was like closing the proverbial barn door a little too late, and the only time that dry gas could help you was *before* the real cold (the Boston weathermen with their glass charts had been drawing icicles on their depictions of incoming fronts for days) and it soaked up any water in your line *before* it had a chance to freeze. But gurgling the contents of the blue-and-yellow can into the tank, holding it in my stinging bare hand, at least I took some satisfaction in the knowledge I was making a try.

It was true. Getting out of Cambridge, which for all intents and purposes was really gritty Boston, then far enough west to a place like Wellesley, was close to dreaming yourself into another part of the world—or even more than that, an entirely different philosophy of the

world. Of course, the campus was at its peak in the
warm weather. Acres and acres of low rolling hills, too-
green lawns, ornamental ponds, winding asphalt roads
with small, tastefully black signs lettered in a sort of
1920s gold glitter telling you where to turn for the different halls. The buildings themselves were in enclaves,
their clusters of spires rising like those of separate vil-
lages above the big leafy trees that puffed pastel blos-
soms in early May or detonated into those golds and
scarlets in late October. But it all had its wintry attrac-
tion now too, white on white, and you noticed how
handsome spruces with snow for their long capes could
be. It was something you missed out on, understandably, when the other trees competed.

I crossed the snow-packed circular drive to the Gothic
portico that was the entrance to Haven Court. I knew
that if any building on the campus represented that look
straight out of the War of the Roses, then indeed this was
it. It rose bigger than the rest in their various ends of the
campus, and the profusion of mullioned windows and
gargoyles had to hold a record here. And it didn't let up
when I entered the overheated air of the front parlor you
had to go through, over the seedy Oriental carpeting and
past the dark paneled walls heavy with bookcases overflowing, to get to the corner cubbyhole for the bell

desk. Alice was only a sophomore, and when she herself
had arrived as a freshman the year before she had no say
in where they would room her. Nevertheless, Haven
Court was the kind of place where Alice belonged and
where she stayed.

It would be good to see her again.

The girl at the bell desk was new, I was sure, snub-
nosed and wearing a heathery cable-knit sweater complete with a bona fide gold circle pin, a touch I hadn't
seen for a while. I liked the way that you could see the
spaghetti of rainbow wires behind the board that had
been pulled away some for repairs and never put back
properly. And I liked to think how via it you could listen
in on any of those girls at any given moment, almost
secretly tune in on what any of them was thinking too.

"For Alice McCall," she said.

"Yes," I said.

"I'll ring her."

"To say you have a caller for Alice McCall-her," I
said with a smile.

It was an old line. I used it too fast before it sank in
that if this girl knew ahead of time who I wanted to
see, then she had probably been on duty enough at
"bells" to have heard me employ the witticism before. I
sat on one of the creaky chairs off in a reading nook—

yes, that oaken thing had a high back carved with heraldic diamonds—and waited. Was there anything better than those minutes after you had called up for a girl, and then sat there comfortably knowing that before long she would materialize, to *greet* you? A clock ticked, I heard a few random notes of what was definitely "Yellow Submarine." They came from the grand piano in the front parlor, and though I couldn't see any of it, I simply pictured some girl on her way through the long room going to the library with all her books, and she just had to stop for a minute to poke out the few keys and happily hear it. It was that beginning part where Ringo —I guess it was—sang about the town where he was born, and the man who sailed the seas telling them all about his life: "In the la-and of sub-ma-rines. . . ."

Actually, I knew that things weren't going too well for Alice herself just then. This last month or so since she had returned from the Midwest, where she had seen her parents individually, had been hard. And after another one of the painful long-distance calls to her mother there the evening before, she phoned me and we decided that it would be better if we canceled our usual Saturday-night date. Instead, I would come out to see her on Sunday, and we could skate together; I could even get in some pond hockey. We could relax.

*   *   *

"Willy, after all, he is my father," Alice said. Sadly.

"I know," I said.

"So what am I supposed to do, go through my whole life pretending that I never had a father? Ignore him completely?"

"No. I mean, yes, what you're doing all makes sense."

"But it's all also hurting my mother so much. I can understand the way she feels, but I just don't think that she's trying to understand the way I feel. But I shouldn't say that. Willy, will you listen to me saying that, with my mother having done everything, just about everything in the whole world, for me."

"Relax."

I kissed her on the forehead.

We were both sitting on the edge of the lumpy bed of her dormitory room on the third floor. She had lucked out, got this room of her own in a draw for "singles" that fall. Alice was five-ten. That was probably why we had met at the Lowell House mixer the year before. (My suddenly going to mixers was precipitated by the rapid split then with Evelyn, who had been the first girl I had ever dated "seriously" and could call a girlfriend, high school included.) If I had any physical attribute it was my height, six-three, but always, admittedly, a

gangly six-three. There was the noise of an undergrad-
uate electric rock band with not more than a half-
dozen basic guitar chords, and there was that reddish
light that they somehow always rigged up for such
functions. We noticed each other because we towered
almost like some other leaf-munching species above the
true sea of bobbing heads, the couples frugging away.

Alice now wore loose corduroy slacks and a bulky
cowl-neck sweater, white. Her long and sleek golden hair
was done in a functional-enough big braid, and she had
on her perfectly round steel-rimmed glasses that made
her blue eyes seem bigger still, huge as a Martian's—in a
pretty way, if that makes any sense. I wondered again if I
would even have made that initial contact with a girl as
handsome as she if it hadn't been for my height. It had
really dealt me the advantage over nearly all the guys at
that mixer that night. I eventually approached her and
tried my best at fast-dancing, something I was never even
passable at (the frug? the pony? who knows), to Wilson
Pickett's "In the Midnight Hour."

"I'm glad you're here," she said, as we currently sat
there together. "I miss you, and it always seems so long
during the week."

"I miss you, too." I kissed her again on the forehead,
lightly, and then right on top where the part gave way

to the flaxen rope as thick as your clenched fist. "I mean, I do."

"He wants me to stay there with him again, during spring break."

"Then do it."

"But my *mother.*"

I hated to see how this was hurting Alice. I knew that how I could help, if in no other way, was to let her talk about it. And maybe that would contribute to her feeling that what she was doing at this point was the right thing, granting it really wasn't contributing *all* that much.

Her parents were both doctors. They married during medical school at Northwestern in Chicago, which, as Alice explained to me, was in the dim downtown of the city and not, like the rest of the university, in Evanston and on the giant plane of blue Lake Michigan. But her mother dropped out shortly afterward when Alice's older sister was born, and then after Alice was born, a few years later, the father abandoned the family for a nurse and went to live with her in his "favorite town" of Pine River, Minnesota; he had spent summers there as a boy. That left Alice's mother and the two girls having to move into a cramped walk-up apartment, while the mother returned to all those labs and all those hours-upon-dragging-hours of an eventual internship in a lying-in hospital that paid poorly. At that time none of Chicago's major general hospitals was willing to take on a woman. (I often wondered if Alice wasn't a bit over-dramatic about those supposed hard times, and it was true that through that trying stretch the household always had a housekeeper *plus* a full-time black cook named Alabama, famous for her strawberry-jam flap-jacks.) Her mother eventually did build up a practice in pediatrics in a downstate town; there, her being a woman couldn't be held against her, simply because they had no option of expressing prejudice and needed *any* doctor. She sent Alice's older sister and Alice to the posh boarding school in Lake Forest (I loved those yearbook pictures of Alice in the school uniform of blazer and tie, the pleated plaid skirt and knee stockings making her look awkward in her tallness, always a little knock-kneed), yet Alice maybe emerged as her favorite. The sis-ter had a hometown boyfriend, so she decided to go to the University of Illinois, and she left to marry the guy halfway through. Meanwhile, Alice was winning the Latin prizes and the cello medals at school. She was admitted to Wellesley, and her mother was very proud of her, satisfied that Alice had become everything that she had expected, and that it had happened with her raising her on her own. I guess it was understandable that now that Alice had seen the father in Pine River, and now that the father had decided that he wanted to fly her there again, spend time with her in his age, do things for her, Alice's mother was hurt. She had turned cool with Alice, and that led to those marathon long-distance calls between them. Like the one full of heavy pauses the evening before. It had left Alice crying and upset enough that she and I decided, as I said, for her not to come into Cambridge for our usual Saturday evening together of dinner, followed by a movie, and then the night itself at the apartment in the gray triple-decker near Central Square that I shared with two other guys who had moved out of Lowell House with me in our senior year.

"I don't want to hurt her," Alice said. "But I don't want to hurt him either."

"Just relax," I said.

I started smooching with her, and she gradually responded. She hugged me hard.

"Oh, sweet Willy, I *have* missed you so."

I started groping further, under that white sweater. Eyes closed, I fingered the little satiny bow on the front of her bra, then cupped the softness of one globe and then the other. We kissed some more, both of us getting huffy.

"We can have cocoa," she said, "and then so much fun when you get back from skating."

"You don't want to skate?" I asked her.

"Taki and I will meet you, OK, around three, on the lake. I haven't done a thing all week, with those telephone calls worrying me so, and I have to finish this stupid team project with her for that stupid philosophy class. Then that way you can play your hockey, and then give Taki and me some professional tips."

"Fine."

"But I don't feel like doing that project, to tell the truth."

She hugged me hard again. She seemed sad again.

"No, you *should* do it. You said that the guy who teaches the course is a pill, right, so no use taking any chances. From the sound of it, he'd love to dock you big if you turned in the thing five minutes late, never mind a week, and it's almost a week overdue, right?"

"I suppose."

Taki was her best friend. She was a girl of Japanese descent from California, and she was entirely soft-voiced and sunny. Even if it was the dead of winter, exam time too at the moment, just the presence of Taki in the room in her peasant blouse (Mexican) and her long "hippie" skirt (the red faded to rose) and her flip-flop sandals (rubber things in which her little feet themselves seemed to ride contentedly) was to make you think that standing there after a knock on the door and Alice opening it, carrying a pile of dense philosophy texts, Taki had come to announce spring. And you remembered how in spring Taki laced her long black hair with white daisies or bluebells, a touch that somebody like cheery Taki could get away with without it seeming any affectation whatsoever.

I gathered up my hockey equipment—manfully for the benefit of the girls?—and headed out, reminding them that I expected to see them there on the ice at three on the dot.

Would there ever be any excuse for what I did next? I suppose I could later say that I wasn't myself. How could anybody be himself in a time like January 1969? If there was any hope for America, it had fizzled the year before when a stubble-faced malcontent shot Martin Luther King and then another one did the same to Bobby Kennedy in that dream of the victory party in the confused reception room of the Los Angeles hotel; at that stage it seemed that everything had grown so crazy that somehow, weirdly, there wasn't even a shock to seeing Jack Kennedy's brother shaggy-haired and spilling a pool of dark blood like that as the cameras flashed—it was inevitable, just a matter of time before it did happen. And not to get carried away with it, but, again, how was I supposed to act? The nightly newsclips on TV showed more and more guys my age being spilled out of teetering helicopters onto the flattened yellow paddy grass, holding their rifles in one hand and their dog tags close to their camouflage T-shirts with the other, running scared for shelter that never seemed to be there. Worse, I had gone to eat in the Lowell House dining room one evening that fall; I noticed on the official house bulletin board the official sheet of house stationery saying that Thomas R. Vliet, Lowell House 1968, had been killed in a parachute-training accident at Fort Benning, Georgia. It maybe wasn't a genuine combat death, but I had never heard anything like the dining room the way it was that evening—or *not* heard anything. No general clamor of laughter, or argument, or simple conversation, so quiet that you could distinctly hear the knives and forks clicking away on the tan plastic compartment plates at the green beans or the gravied pot roast, and chairs squeaking on the floor as guys got up to head with their trays to the conveyor belt in the rear. In six months I would graduate, and despite all your protest, average time on the street for a college graduate before induction (physicals included) was about sixty days in 1969.

The world was crazy.

On the other hand, there was no excuse. True, I loved Alice, and her concern for her parents reminded me again how she was somebody special, somebody rare. But leaving Haven Court in the cold, lugging my hockey stuff, I turned up the collar on my pea coat, and I knew even then that I was going directly to see if my old girlfriend, Evelyn, was in her dormitory room that afternoon. There was no convincing myself that I just happened to stop by, seeing I was on my way to the big college lake and that lake was sort of near her dormitory, Lange Hall.

Lange Hall.

Truly an architectural mistake, it was one of the few attempts at modernity at Wellesley. It was a place probably designed by some famous avant-garde Finn in the fifties, but looking, if you were honest, like just another one of the unheard-of number of streamlined grade schools built at about the same time everywhere in America to handle the onslaught of baby-boomers. Apparently nobody really wanted to live in Lange and you just ended up there. Nobody except for somebody like Evelyn; she thought it was so bad it was good. I asked for her at the Lange bell desk. I sat on one of the sleek light-wood benches and looked at the giant potted rubber trees. The lobby wasn't even on the first floor, but underground, as if you had to make a tunneling entrance to the building. Strange.

I heard the elevator at the end of the long flagstone runway of a hall hum to a stop. I watched as Evelyn came down that stretch the way she always did—slow, dragging her feet some. That was the way she inevitably approached in the course of the year we had dated, while both sophomores. It ended the following fall. I had come out there then to pick her up, and she honestly confessed to me that she had been with a "boy" in Milan most of that summer in Europe. She had taken art courses at Milan's university, and there had been a pregnancy, and there had been an abortion in rainy Sweden. She traveled to Stockholm alone on rattling third-class trains, using a girlfriend's doctored Eurail pass; the boy, Italian and an architecture grad student, had disappeared pretty fast when their problem developed. Evelyn liked to tease me about my Catholicism, but she also always saw it as something that could be "interesting" because it was mysterious, for me, anyway. In any case, she knew that her misadventures over the summer would be tough for me to come to terms with—and it was true. For her, she considered the whole thing an experience she had to go through, and often messes like that could be "interesting" too. Evelyn was constantly thinking about the interesting, and she constantly wished to simply forget the hangups of a place like Wellesley, forget the hangups of her parents especially. (They lived in a modernistic redwood house in Darien, Connecticut, about as ritzy a suburb as you could get. Her father was a respected New York trial attorney. He wore turtlenecks and velour bellbottoms, drove an MG sports car, and took off sailing with her brothers in their ketch for weeks on end; frankly, he never appeared to me to have any hangups.) Evelyn painted and painted, and she would say that she supposed her work wasn't very good. But those paintings—detached eyes staring from murkily surreal backgrounds, etc.—to me were quite accomplished. I felt a sentimental rush about all the time we had spent together, now as I watched her coming down that corridor.

She wasn't that tall. She had high cheekbones and full lips. And if you looked at her from a distance like this, in a black sweater and black jeans, you would tell somebody: "I bet that girl is some kind of an artist. A poet, or a painter, or something." That walk, those feet dragging, her smile alone saying what she often said outright: "Can you believe I actually am at a college like this?" or, "Can you believe they even *have* colleges like this?"

Evelyn was so intelligent. Evelyn was rare.

"Willy, what did you do to your hair?"

Her voice was slow, and she could sound whisper-
ingly sexy saying something as simple as that. She had
dark eyes.

"Short, huh," I said.

I always cultivated what I fancied was a Keith Richard
shag. But then I happened to try the barbershop on
Dunster Street because I got a tip that the proprietor
still believed in the dollar-fifty cut. (The scholarship
dough wasn't entirely great, and even figuring in my
earnings from working as a framing carpenter in the
summers in Maine, plus my father's help, money was
always tight.) I think the barber probably stuck to that
rock-bottom price just to exact a little sadistic fun on
what he must have seen as all of us pinko Hah-vahd
lightweights. I should have known I was in big-league
trouble as soon as I sat on one of the sagging, chrome-
armed chairs to wait and pretended I was interested in
the *Record-American* and then the gun-and-ammo magazines, the only reading supplied.

In a way that time away from Evelyn hadn't passed.
Seeing each other again was nothing more than an easy
exchange about my lousy haircut. I was still completely
in love with her too.

Evelyn shared a suite of rooms with a few other girls.
They were gone for the weekend, and Evelyn had decid-

ed to use the quiet of being alone to paint. The suite was on top of Lange. It had originally been intended as a tutor's quarters, and now it went to seniors as maybe a consolation for having lived in Lange for four years. The sunlight was blindingly strong, with the big picture windows up there overlooking so much reflecting snow on the roofs of the dorm's lower levels and then on the hills beyond; the brightness had broken out in earnest suddenly, the day's gray long gone. We talked about what we had done lately, old friends and what they were doing. We drank some wine she took from the grumbling little portable refrigerator. And amid the aroma of linseed oil and her paints and brushes spread out around an easel, we eventually made love in that brighter-than-brightness. I should add that Evelyn, despite her Bohemian code, needed a good measure of coaxing and convincing from me. She knew I had been dating another girl at Haven Court, though I kept saying, lying, that the relationship wasn't serious and I was presently out at Wellesley only to get in some skating and escape Cambridge, where everybody was going a little bonkers with exams.

She cried afterwards, apologizing for it, but not able to help herself and softly crying some more.

I remembered then what I had repressed for so long—

how she had cried a lot during our breakup after her summer in Italy. But I didn't have time to stay around and soothe her now. It was two thirty-seven according to the little flipping black slabs of her bedside clock radio, and if Alice and Taki were due on the ice at three, I had to make it look like I had been playing strenuous hockey for a couple of hours when they arrived.

There is a rare element about hockey. As soon as you step onto the ice, anybody who knows anything about the game can peg you right away. It's not the same when a guy shows up on a dusty sandlot for touch football or at a grassy city park to see if anybody can use him in an in-progress softball game. It's all in the simple stride, smooth and from the hip, and how you look just so god-damn relaxed wearing the big battered leather gloves (about the only protection that is really proper for pond play, and maybe shin pads) and holding your stick with-out being conscious of it, the swooshing blades of your CCMs on the hard surface as natural as anybody else's slapping sneaker soles on pavement. Sure, any insider can easily conclude: "That guy's played hockey before, pretty seriously too." It was always a nice moment for me. I had indeed played for our city high school in Maine that made it to the state tournament in my junior year. I was also, to be honest, backup defense, a reserve. Nevertheless, it definitely helped me get the academic scholarship to Harvard, where I spent nearly the whole of my freshman year in the dreamed-of crimson uniform on the bench. I did see about six minutes of play when the coach let some of us in, if only to make us feel good, against an unknown prep school named Lennox—after we "frosh" had a dozen-goal lead on them. Hockey at Harvard was light-years out of my league; fortunately, maybe, so I wasn't as much as tempted to waste my time with it after that initial, and butt-atrophying, season.

Out there on the ice at the moment, I noticed a couple of them in the ongoing pickup game eyeing me. The players were a mixed bunch. Some high-schoolers in their Bruins or Maple Leafs jerseys, some guys about college age most likely visiting girls that Sunday, and some older sorts, suburbanites with a group affection for those expensive white wool Mackinaw coats, probably Boston lawyers and doctors and brokers, who were well aware of how old they were and wisely hung back to relax on defense. Meanwhile, everybody else raced around in the messy flow of slamming sticks and loud shouts for coverage, passing, and more complicated ideas like "Set it up!" that didn't have a chance in a game of this ilk. One side took me on.

My first time with the puck I launched into some wild wheeling and reversing. I lost everybody in my long, egomaniacal rush, finally cruising in to tuck the puck in one corner of the goal defined by two pine logs, smack between the legs of the worried goalie; he was one of those older parties wearing—pathetically, wobblingly—black figure skates. There came friendly charges of "Ringer!" from the opposition and then a rain of "Right ons!" from those on my team, surprisingly well versed as a bunch in the vernacular of the day. Red and huffing, I skated slowly back to announce I would volunteer for defense for a while after that. But I did feel strong, confident, and wasn't it true, I *still* had my moves, and I . . . that was definitely the last time I was to feel good that afternoon.

Because just then I spotted Alice and Taki getting up from a log on the shore after having laced on their skates. They weren't exactly expert themselves. Alice had done a little skating in Illinois, but not much, and Taki from California had bought her first pair of skates only a couple of weeks before. On the ice, they laughed, stumbling in something like a waltz together to maintain at least the idea of balance. *What had I done.*

"Willy!" Alice called, excited. I waved back.

"I think that one run was all I was good for," I told

the high-school kid who was now on defense with me. I was still short of breath. "I might just call it a day."

"That was some skating, mister," the kid said.

I stared at his dumb face set right atop the big maple leaf on the chest of his Toronto jersey. I wondered if anybody had ever called me "mister" before.

"Willy!" Alice shouted again.

Alice wore a taupe wool dress coat, midi-length, the big gold braid trailing out from a purple ski hat tugged nearly over her eyes. Taki, her teeth like shiny shells, smiled and shivered in the cold that could really bite when the wind gusted. She still wore the long cotton hippie skirt, and her orange down parka seemed inflated, as if she had on a life preserver. I joined them.

"How do you skate backwards?" Alice said to me.

"How do you skate *frontwards*," Taki said. We all laughed. I had to force it a bit.

"You look tired," Alice said. She pecked a kiss on my reddened cheek. "You've been killing yourself out here for almost three hours, and now you should spend some time with us."

"Three hours," I said. "I guess you're right."

The day had turned steely again. Just a band of late-afternoon pink glowing along the hills gave the sole evidence that the sun had even broken through earlier.

The trio of us headed far down the ice. We kept near the shore at first, past drooping, yellow-fingered weeping willows, then cut right out for the center of the lake and pushed on toward the opposite side. Long seasoning cracks echoed like kettledrums, and exactly in the middle, where the surface had frozen last and, so, before the snow had come, the girls were amazed at how black it was in its clarity. And the way you could indeed look straight through it, like a lens, to actually see what was a fine display of unbelievably long green weeds far below.

"Wow," Taki said.

"I'll say," Alice said.

It must have taken us a good half-hour for that trip across, including stopping for the sights along the way. We found a tiny sheltered inlet with a dock where a hillock blocked the wind, which was dying, anyway. The branches there were coated with frost, many of the brushy trees sprouting right up through the ice. Alice said she remembered one of her few times skating as a kid and being in the same kind of wintry grotto.

"Trees, or bushes, just like this. We called it Fantasyland, because it looked like it was right out of Walt Disney. Or maybe it was Wonderland, as in Winter Wonderland. I don't know. Anyway, the boys would grab the girls' hats and go buzzing off into the maze of trees like this, and we squealed that we would *kill* them if we ever caught them, happily, you know. It was so much fun."

After another half-hour of shivering, though always smiling, Taki left. Alice and I didn't last much longer ourselves. Everything Alice said to me as she clung to my arm on our long haul back seemed to make it more painful. It was as if suddenly I felt badly about *everything*. Not just what I had done to Alice that afternoon in my cheating and how Evelyn crying, hurt, had made it worse, but also the fact that I hadn't even called my father since I returned from Christmas vacation in Maine, and the fact that I had given up on my honors thesis in English—what did I have to add to the mountain of cerebral babble that already existed about Joyce?—and jumped ship on that after working so hard with my kind, concerned tutor to qualify for the honors track. (Easy pickings for the well-trained prep-school kids, not all that easy for somebody who went to a high school in Maine where half of the sad students still talked close to a broken English in their French Canadian accents.) The very fact that the Valiant was having engine problems seemed to be my fault, another thing gone wrong that traced back to my spinelessness.

"I'm so glad you're here," Alice said. "I do mean that so, you know."

"I know," I said. *What had I done.*

Back at her little dormitory room, Alice made the instant cocoa on a hot plate set up in the window alcove. The room had yellow walls and big posters she had brought from Chicago that advertised the summer music concerts at Ravinia. A fine cellist, Alice loved Ravinia. The red Mexican throw rug was little more than a blanket on the oak floor.

We smooched. She tasted of the chocolate's sugar, like a kid would, maybe. Sure enough, I picked up where I had left off when I had arrived there at noon. In one way that felt long ago, in a distant era well before the wine (not detectable, I trusted) and my visit with Evelyn, and before the stretch of skating in the cold— even if that stretch didn't include the three hours or so of hard play and *six* goals for me, as I readily lied to Alice. In another way it was as if no time had passed whatsoever, and cad that I was, I continued under her sweater, pushing it up as she eased back to the bed, my tongue on one pink nipple in loops and loops until it was hard and glistening with my saliva, and then my tongue on the other in the same loops and loops until it was hard and glistening with my saliva. To balance off such symmetry, I put my tongue in the warm knot of her navel, her downy stomach amber in the low light. The silver-painted radiator clanked and crazily hissed.

We made love twice. After the second time, she cried, but she said it was because she was so happy, so in love with me that she couldn't believe it. And she didn't know how she would *ever* have made it through this sadness concerning her parents if it hadn't been for me always being there to listen, to let her talk about it.

"You're so nice to me," she said. In the dark we almost couldn't see each other. I didn't say anything. "You really are."

I wished that Evelyn hadn't cried. I really wished that Alice hadn't cried. I wished I wasn't me. That evening we studied together in her room, had grilled cheese-and-tomato sandwiches she made on the hot plate.

Starting the Valiant was probably a sign, because what eventually happened was kind of amazing, in a way.

Having left Haven Court, I sat on the car's seat that was like a cold cement slab. I turned the key to hear the usual Skil-saw screech of the starter motor. I felt the uneasy rumble as the AMP and TEMP lights continued to flash red in the slow chugging; they finally extinguished when the engine worked through a couple of rough revs. But not a bad start, everything considered. I gently maneuvered down the steep incline of the narrow lane, the snow there as solid as tundra, and continued along the winding central campus road, which in truth wasn't any wider than a side street. I began to sense a whisper of warmth from the heater by the time I got to that stretch of Route 16 that became the Village of Wellesley's main street: its closed drugstores and dress shops and bookstores with the miniature Mount Vernon facades, then the intersection and the signal light, suspended above the nonexistent traffic, slow-blinking its yellow in the night—a night that was absolutely calm and deep blue. The car was maybe running smoothly after that warm-up; the dry gas maybe *had* worked. There was some traffic before long, even then at quarter past twelve. It was obviously a lot of guys from Harvard who had been out to see girls that evening, presently heading back after visiting hours ended at midnight. I suspected a ninety-year-old geezer was heading up this de facto convoy, and there must have been a line of close to a dozen of us behind him by the time we hit the stretch of shadowy residential Colonials and Victorians before you got to the Turnpike entrance in West Newton. I had no question about taking the Turnpike at this point. The way I was feeling, the trick was going to be to just pay the couple of tolls for the fast ride to Cambridge, just wrap this day up and try to forget it.

The slow-mover was a long black fifties Cadillac, four-door and funereal, old enough to be one of those models where you pressed the tiny round red reflector on the taillight assembly built into one fin, for that whole thing to spring open on a hinge and give access to the hidden gas cap. He at last turned off right after the huge hospital. With him out of the way, the rest of us could have been at the starting line of a Southern cracker's stock-car race, and the entire parade, Harvard decals on the rear windows included, charged hard into the next mile or so and then the quick curve of the Turnpike access ramp. Where there was a backup, some commotion.

It seemed that each time the car at the head of the convoy would reach the unmanned automatic toll kiosk, which asked for only a dime to enter here, the driver would stop for a while and then accelerate with more than a normal blast. It also seemed that in this case somebody was outside, and halfway there I recognized him. He had a wonderful halo of curly blond hair, what was affectionately called a "Jewish Afro" back then, a short, stocky guy who I remembered from the big demonstrations that fall on the wide steps of Widener

Library or from other spots around campus too, selflessly passing out leaflets to guys coming back from the house dining rooms, sometimes in the pouring rain. He grinned. He held in his hand, as if it were a revolutionary's rifle, the black-and-white-striped arm of the toll gate, and it looked as if the long thing had been snapped off clean near its base; the bright wood innards where it broke shone in a zigzag. Guys would brake their cars for a couple of minutes as they talked with him, then he would theatrically wave each through in a sweep of his free arm. I figured it was his own Volks Beetle, psychedelic spray-painted, parked in the side lane. I followed the brake lights of the car ahead of me, my dime ready. I cranked down the window.

"Forget it, man," he said. "Nobody pays."

"What?" I said

"It's all a rip-off, anyway, paying to use roads, roads that are for the public, the people." He said that last word with a definite capital "P."

"You ran into it?"

"Not me. Some big truck, a semi that skidded some. It's icy, be careful."

"It's only a dime," I said.

I got ready to toss the coin in the white vinyl basket. He reached out to stop me.

"Go, man. It's liberated. We're liberated. We're free. This is the way it's all going to start! Come on!" He was close to dancing in his excitement. "Come *on*!"

I didn't know about the revolution, with a capital "R." But it did feel good just cruising past that toll, then onto the six salt-dusted lanes, where there was no traffic. The panel lights glowed green, the orange speedometer needle worked up to nearly seventy. And in a way I knew fully well right then that, nah, this time next year I wouldn't be lugging a mess kit and fifty pounds of artillery in a steaming foreign country in a meaningless war, forced to shoot at somebody I didn't want to shoot at—or, worse, have *him* shoot at *me*. And what was the big deal, after all, about my behavior on that day out in the other world of Wellesley? I was glad I had seen Evelyn (I would never know what eventually became of her, and today, over twenty-five years later, I guess I will never know), and I was even gladder I had seen Alice. (I do know what happened to her, and when she fell in love with a handsome young Boston banker the following fall and jilted me to marry him, it took me, at that time working for one ridiculous weekly newspaper after another in dead Vermont towns, a couple of years to come out of it.)

On that freeway, however, guilt had been left behind, somewhere in all that snow and all those ever-so-quiet woods surrounding a women's college, where I liked to think that now all the girls in all the little rooms were softly sleeping in the dark, completely lost, as their silver radiators continued to clank out whispery contentment for the green twilit parks and proverbial mansions of many golden chambers that we commonly call sweet dreams.

The glow of Cambridge and Boston was amber in the distance. I laughed out loud, because I still couldn't get over that poor guy bouncing around like that in his surplus-store parka and bellbottom jeans with peace-symbol patches, at least one man convinced the Revolution had at long last arrived.

The Valiant ran like a top. I had this feeling that if I switched on the radio it would be, yes, "Yellow Submarine."

Additional Consideration

I

It seems egregious that in the plethora of available study and commentary on the role of shooting in the game, there has been almost complete neglect of The Sleep Shot.

A brief review of sources commonly relied on more than emphasizes the full range of this oversight, the troubling depth of it as well. That staple of the coach's instructional bookshelf, Brown,[1] has introduced many a student from the Maritimes to Vancouver, from Maine to Minnesota,[2] to the commonly accepted categorization for what might be seen as the Ancient Triumvirate: The Forehand (with mirroring backhand); The Snap Shot; and The Slap Shot. How sound are those little boxed, black-and-white photographs of the properly equipped player in the no-name jersey that illus-

1. Don Hayes, *Ice Hockey,* from Brown Publishers' Physical Education Activities Series, Dubuque, Iowa, 1972, plus earlier editions.
2. One envisions the day when the United States will not be axed in two, when boys playing Pee Wee and Midget and Bantam, like the NHL itself, will truly stretch from America's sea to shining sea.

trate form in Brown and that many a boy has pored long hours over in hopes of perfecting his own play. And how any one of us can remember to this day the wisdom of Brown we were made to repeat almost as a mantra by our coaches—yes, "both arms and wrists contribute to shooting"—and how many a student flipped fast through the pages of that surely well-worn little gem, willing to skip the plea of always to remember the backhand in the coming age of the banana curve, plus the heavy emphasis on follow-through for any shot, just to get to the near-forbidden heart of the matter indeed, that talk of The Slap:

"One of the newer offensive weapons in hockey is the slap shot. There is little doubt that this is the most spectacular shot in the game. This is probably due to the uncertainty of where it is going, the speed of the puck, and the cannonading noise when it hits the boards." (Cannonading! The very boom of the word!) "Unfortunately, like most new ideas, there is a tendency to oversell it, thus we are now experiencing a period of overuse to the detriment of goal scoring." (A run to the kitchen to find the cherished *Webster's* Mom kept in the second drawer beneath the counter with her little yellow pads for shopping lists, to look up the word "detriment" and know that if The Slap was *bad,* then it was also what we heady young rebels *wanted* more than anything else!) "The primary value of this shot is the speed with which it travels, thus it becomes a long-distance scoring play."

All told in Brown, there are eight full pages and eleven of those inset photographs to illustrate the various points established concerning shooting, a rather sizable amount of the text when one considers that the volume itself in its 1972 edition is a scant sixty-four pages overall.

And, again, not a mention of The Sleep Shot.

II

Two other valued texts make no attempt to remedy the situation either.

The popular rule book, Chadwick,[3] shows its usual readable chattiness when it comes to matters of the stick, and subsequently shooting. It is very easy to understand how Chadwick's basic intimacy has made it the referee's pillowside companion that it is today, replacing the earlier, more direct compilation of such rule-book material, sometimes simply in no more than

3. Bill Chadwick, *Illustrated Ice Hockey Rules*, Garden City, New York, 1976.

a mimeographed, stapled-together booklet.[4] Add to that the paperback's physical attractiveness, with the full-color photograph of the crouching ref in the wild fray of blurring red uniforms on the ice during heated play on the glossy cover, then the way that Chadwick employs his direct "problem and solution" presentation, and you have a package that can't help but appeal to those men in stripes. Here is the lead-in to Section 3, Rule 20B, concerning the matter of curvature of the stick:

THE BLADE
Problem

When he played in the NHL, Bobby Hull had a curved blade on the end of his hockey stick that made his already awesome slap shot one of the most dangerous weapons in the history of hockey. When Hull's crooked blade connected on the slap shot, the puck would soar and dip crazily. "How can you stop that thing?" asked one angry goalie. "You never know where it's going. It's like trying to catch a knuckleball that's going a hundred miles an hour. The damned thing is going to kill somebody one of these days."

4. As a note, and to afford the fairer sex equal time (fairer, but often just as exciting, an opinion based on my own attendance at ladies' matches in my Potsdam, New York), the standard rule book for women's play in the United States remains the concise *Ice Hockey Rules,* compiled by the National Association for Girls and Women in Sport, Reston, Virginia, 1980.

Solution

> Eventually, legislation was adopted restricting the cur-
> vature of the stick's blade to one-half inch—quite a bit less
> than the hook Hull was using.

Again, no denying the lure of that prose itself—the crystal clarity and the aforementioned chattiness—but while speaking of the omnipresent Slapper does Chadwick ever turn his attention to The Sleep Shot?

Similarly, one may go to the other end of the spectrum. Journey almost as far away from the beloved Brown of schoolboys or the chatty Chadwick of judicious referees, into the world of the scholarship to which so many of us have tirelessly devoted our academic lives, and the situation fails to improve an iota. We as a group admittedly remain breathless at the sheer scope of the groundbreaking research in the Landry and Orban volume.[5] And though my purpose in this paper is to call for additional consideration of The Sleep Shot at last, I myself cannot pass up the opportunity to point out some of the true fruits of the solid, selfless research contained within. One of the more intriguing papers for

---

5. *Ice Hockey: Research, Development and New Concepts,* papers from the International Congress of Physical Activity Sciences, a conference held in Quebec City, July 11-16, 1976, edited by Fernand Landry, Ph.D. and William R. Orban, Ph.D., Miami, 1978, a publication of Symposia Specialists, Incorporated.

me in that collection, with its total of fifteen papers, has to be "Inter- and Intragame Alterations in Selected Blood Parameters During Ice Hockey Performance" by that tireless trio of lab-lovers at the University of Waterloo—H. J. Green, M. E. Houston, and J. A. Thomson—and a similar tip of the mortarboard must go to the study of equipment represented best for me therein by that dazzling duo from Université Laval, Benoit Roy and Conrad Lauzier: "Caractéristiques dynamiques des patins de hockey à l'impact de ron-delles." And, of course, investigation into shooting itself could very well approach its apex, scientifically speaking, in the volume's paper that comes to us from our colleagues in the sunny Southland, W. R. Halliwell and J. L. Gropell and T. Ward at the Movement Science Program, Florida State University, Tallahassee, Florida: "A Kinematic Analysis of the Snap Shot in Ice Hockey as Executed by Professional Hockey Players." They toiled hard to put under the microscope members from what was then the Atlanta Flames squad, employing strict mathematical charting that would make even kindly old Dr. Einstein proud. Consider this:

> In the execution of both the high and low snap shots, the displacement data clearly showed that after reversing direction, the upper hand continued to move

away from the target, in the opposite direction to which the lower hand was moving. Thus, the upper and lower hands passed each other and thereby momentarily occupied the same spatial position just prior to the impact. At impact, the upper hand had moved behind the lower hand. Although this distance was rather minimal for the low snap shot (1.84 cm) it was considerably greater for the high snap shot (6.43 cm).

Impressive, certainly amazing—Bravo!

I suppose one could argue that a bonus in their triumph is that their study on shooting focuses on The Snap Shot for once; which means The Snap can still hold its resilient own in a time when everybody wants to talk and talk and talk about The Slap Shot (so *proud* the dear departed coaches of our youth would be to see that respect for The Snap). But, and nevertheless, doesn't The Sleep Shot deserve at least one reference, a single mention?

III

Here is the transcript of a tape taken from the nearly three hundred hours of recordings that I have made in my own research into The Sleep Shot over the last thirteen years at Clarkson University:[6]

6. The subject was male, forty-seven years old.

"I left work early, around two P.M.[7] I knew that the
visiting hours didn't begin until four on the dot, but I
didn't let that bother me. Because this wasn't a period
in my life when I was going to let a little thing stand in
my way. A little thing like time, and the ridiculousness
of what the glowing red sticks said on my digital clock
at home, or what was said by the loping frilled hands of
the big city hall clock with its Roman numerals—none
of what any of them had to tell me meant much to me
right then. I was maybe outside of that, or I wanted so
much to think I was. I won't say a lot about my job,
except that it was a boring, secure one. If that was
something I had held against myself earlier in life, a
failure of sorts, it was something I valued in the course
of my long, drawn-out divorce, when I knew my job
was at least one front on which I was at least on rela-
tively stable ground. It was late April, the way that a
rainy day like that can look lavender, and the wind-
shield wipers of my car flopped back and forth like
sluggish metronomes. Of course I knew that I *better*
start thinking about time. Because those nurses could
be tough in enforcing the visiting-hours regulations,

7. I should point out that throughout my research I strove to maintain full
anonymity for the subjects. I requested that he or she narrate with as little
specific detail as possible concerning geographic location, etc., even avoiding
pinpointing occupation, as happens here.

and with my being two hours early, the whole trick would be not to identify myself as a ready mark who they could easily frighten away. Which is to say, it was almost like when I played hockey in high school, and back then so much mattered on how you carried yourself, how you tried to adopt a swagger on skates so that anybody else out there on the ice saw you as somebody not to fool around with. I parked the car in the lot of the hospital that was a few miles outside our downtown, there in a patch of suburban woods. I walked across the asphalt, through the automatic sliding doors that hummed open for me. The first big mistake, I knew, would be to linger, to ask the volunteer in candy stripes at the information desk what the visiting hours actually were, try to slip myself in by playing dumb, smiling. I had had that backfire on me before, and now I didn't even think about it as an option. I simply walked right past her, right past the little boutique too that savagely overcharged for its get-well cards and large assortment of what I had long before learned were hopelessly stale granola bars. I took the chugging elevator, alone, up to 3-West. I got a bit dizzy the way I always did there, just to inhale that thick overheated air with its smell of ether, some piney disinfectant mixed in, and I maneuvered my way through the maze of abandoned carts overflowing with mountains of used linen. I saw the central island of the floor's nurses' station looming like a fortress up beyond me, and the seemingly miles of glossily buffed yellow linoleum to cover to get there—then to get *past* it. But that particular day the island proved no problem. There was only one youngish nurse on duty. She was a pretty redhead with too much lipstick for a hospital job, and she was chatting with a tall, good-looking resident doctor, who might have been Indian or Pakistani, as if the guy were a true hero, Eisenhower Arriving. The older nurse with the bulldog jaw, a woman I will call Sullivan, was nowhere to be seen, luckily, and I kept on moving, past the open doors to the other rooms along the corridor. There, inside, the lights were out in some of the rooms, in others they were on, milkily dim fluorescent illumination, and in too many of the rooms one of those miniature rental televisions on a complicated steel arm gadget suspending it overhead crackled away with the usual canned applause of an afternoon talk show, or whatever. The challenge here was not to confront that kind of particularly saddening obstacle head-on, but attempt, as hard as you could, not to be caught staring in at any one of them. Maybe a young guy in traction, or an old woman in a loose johnny and tired skin like a crumpled paper bag she had shrunk out of. The challenge, or trick, was above all to avoid thinking about them, and to stare straight ahead. Because be it somebody young or old or anywhere in between, the eyes would look at you and they would say with an utter lostness that had everything to do with time and however long they had been there or however long they would be there (I guess I couldn't forget those glowing red digital sticks, or the big hands on the city hall clock inching around and around), eyes that could drill right through you and almost whisper: 'Look at you out there walking on that yellow linoleum, you who are able to just stroll in here and then, whenever you want, stroll back out again, as if you're the King of Norway himself. How lucky you are, how goddamn lucky you are.' On the other hand, if they *only knew,* as the old saw goes, and for all intents and purposes who was really *in* the hospital and who was really *out of* the hospital, sprung clear free of Floor 3-W, was relative. It was all relative, and then some. Nevertheless, passing the rooms I didn't linger any longer than I had at the information desk or the nurses' station, and before I knew it I was beyond them as well, and I was at Room 317. Where my father was dying. If my stomach had performed its somersault as I first breathed in that whiff of the Hospital Aroma earlier, it did half-dozen such tumbles to see again the lettering of my father's name in bold Magic Marker under the clear plastic sleeve on the door casing, then to head in and see my father himself—my still-handsome, eighty-two-year-old father with his shock of white hair and fine straight nose—to see him hooked up to the tubes and the beeping electronic monitors, as he lay flat on his back in the cranked-up stainless-steel bed. *Still* sleeping. Because for the twelve days he had been in Room 317 now, he had been sleeping nearly continuously. The doctor, safe behind the protecting blank lenses of his perfectly round glasses with horn rims, he wasn't at all as talkative as that resident who had probably been lining up dinner at a French restaurant later with the redheaded nurse, and he had told me frankly a few days before: 'He won't leave here alive, of course. I'm surprised that he's hanging on, and originally I wouldn't have given him the week-plus he has lasted already. There's no need of me deceiving you. You'll come to terms with it, in time. Believe me.' I didn't want to believe him, yet I did appreciate his leveling with me. My brother, however, did believe him, and I think my brother, and especially his wife, just wanted me to agree to finally approving of the cutting off of all the misnamed 'life support,' letting him pass on. But my brother had been away from our city for a long time before he came back there for the week with his entire family, to stay in a motel now that my father was hospitalized and in such serious condition. And what I told myself was that as good as the intentions of my concerned, practical brother were, he had been away altogether too long to know my father as well as I did. You see, with my own marriage a bust and my own two daughters off with their remarried mother in Cleveland,[8] I had spent a lot of time with my father in the past several years, the years during which he was bedridden and had to be taken care of by his housekeeper/nurse, seeing that my mother had died when I was still in college. I drove him around on weekends, I wheeled him through the malls where the security guards supply you with a wheelchair if you ask, and through the new home-supply depot too. We watched the Pirates games in the summer and the Penguins in the winter. It gets complicated here, and I suppose that knowing how much zip my father had often shown in his invalid's condition for those bedridden years and having seen him bounce

8. Cleveland, certainly, is not the city mentioned in the transcript, as taped on September 11, 1993. Occasionally, as happens here, the subject did slip and mention a specific place, and I entered a change to assure anonymity, as I also did with the references right below this to the two professional sports teams.

back from a couple of dangerous health scares before, I wasn't about to let him just 'pass on.' I suppose too—as I said, this turns complicated—I suppose I feared that I was a failure in my father's eyes: my being a guy whose wife had left him and now lived with a whiplash lawyer whose name was a household word in Cleveland because of his television ads—he made more in a month, probably, than I would ever have a chance of making in a year—my also being a guy who finally realized that he could forget about ever being close to his two daughters again, now that the girls were away and exposed daily to the Big Feature Production that built on the endless script of my wife telling the girls still one more time of my spinelessness and unreliability, even general stupidity. You see, I had to once and for all remedy at least this immediate situation, and if my wife and daughters were gone, I could write that off, but as to my father I had to tell him the things that I had been meaning to tell him and always thought I would have the chance to tell him. True, there had been plenty of opportunity to do it, and, true, it would have been easy enough to have done it in all of that driving around together we had logged. Or, on one of those evenings when his housekeeper/nurse was off and I showed up to cook the two of us nothing better than a couple of frozen turkey dinners—we always goofed around while eating them, claiming they weren't half bad, even if their being loaded with salt left the two of us having to down a gallon or so of water each before our TV-watching in earnest began at seven or so. But I didn't tell him then. And, wouldn't you know it, the single time of the year I had to go out of our city for my job just happened to be when the EMS unit with its pulsating red roof beacon was called to his house by the housekeeper/nurse, depositing him there in Room 317. And there in Room 317, I still didn't do it. I tried to arrive for the evening meal every day, when he sometimes would wake. I knew that the kids they had working the underpaid, by-the-hour jobs to deliver the meals to the rooms would make no attempt to feed him, help him eat, and I believed that if I could spoon into him some of the jello or some of the melting chocolate ice cream or some of the oily chicken-broth soup, half cold, I might prove the doctor totally wrong in his claim that my father could survive *only* with nourishment from the intravenous drip. And a couple of evenings I did manage to get him to eat a little. And a couple of evenings he stayed awake in bed after that for a while—I pulled up beside his bed the excuse for an easy chair, and on the edge of the thing's salmon-colored vinyl cushion I chat-

ted with him about other things. Or I chatted the best
I could, between the interruptions. Because in the bed
next to him there was a lonely bald guy with one leg
who had spent most of his life in the navy, long retired.
Eavesdropping on us and desiring some companionship
himself, he would hear me mention somebody and he
would go on about how it reminded him of somebody
he had been with in the navy, or he would hear me
mention something and, yeah, he had to blabber how
that reminded him of something that had happened in
the navy, the Seabees, specifically. And then there was
that day. And what I realized in my office that day,
what I knew when I started out over a full two hours
before visiting hours even began, was that I had to tell
my father and I had to tell him now—there was no
time (time, what I thought I was outside of, but of
course nobody ever, ever is), no time whatsoever to
waste. The navy guy had shipped out that morning,
feeling great, apparently, and the bed where he had
been was empty and made up with a thin bright-gold
blanket, but that made no difference. Because when I
arrived so early in hopes of catching my father awake,
he was sleeping. And then when the meal was brought
and eventually taken away, my father was sleeping, and
when my brother and sister-in-law came in with their

own screaming brood my father was sleeping, sleeping as well when they left at seven-thirty. Visiting hours ended at eight, and there would be no toying around with Sullivan now, that big linebacker of a woman. She had gotten word from the redhead on duty earlier, I guess, that I had snuck in early, and she had already thoroughly chewed me out for that major transgression. She now seemed to be getting a kick out of cruising the yellow-linoleum corridor, padding back and forth beyond the door, as she checked histrionically, for my benefit, her wristwatch—it was a jumbo black plastic thing, like one of those contraptions sold to deep-sea divers and surely guaranteed to function a full forty fathoms or more down into the real depths of Sullivan's own miserableness. My father slept, breathing in and breathing out. Sullivan passed by a couple of more times. And my father slept, breathing in and breathing out, noisily. I paced around Room 317 some. What if my father died later that evening? What if the call came through to me later, back in the loneliness of my own shadowy apartment, at three or four into the morning? What if this proved to be the last evening I would ever be with him while he remained part of this planet, still alive? I had to try something. And if my carrying myself confidently into the corridors of the hospital earlier had evoked a memory of my own days as a high-school athlete, that wonderful ice hockey, then what I did next was to try what almost could be called The Sleep Shot, an idea probably stemming from the memory of hockey too.[9] I was desperate, as I have said, I had been there for close to six hours, and I myself had consumed nothing more than a cup of metallic-tasting black coffee and a sticky bun I took two bites out of in the empty cafeteria in the basement. I was outright scared and rattled *and* desperate. I knew I would feel worse, more guilt-plagued, if I missed this last opportunity to tell him, this final chance to connect with him while he was still where the doctor didn't want to admit that he still was—like I said, still *among* us. I went up to the bed. I leaned down to kiss him on his hot cheek, and I passed my hand over his sweaty forehead, to push back his boyish white forelock a bit. I leaned over him again. I started to whisper aloud into his ear, and I guess that I let go with my Sleep Shot: 'I don't want you to die. I want you always to live, always be with me. Or at least I want you to wake up, for me to tell you what I have never properly told you—that I love you more than my own flesh itself, my hand before

9. While I present only this one complete transcript in this paper, I should point out that this subject, as did most others, would repeatedly use the conditional when referring to The Sleep Shot. More on this finding will be presented and explored in Section IV.

me, my nose. You gave me everything, the boat at fourteen when other boys didn't have runabout boats, and the sports car in college when other boys certainly didn't have TR-3s. And if things came easy to me, if you maybe worried later in your life that you made a mistake early on and your generosity had ruined me, made life too easy for me and deprived me of the drive to finish up at that second-rate law school I somehow did get into, the drive to finally grow up and stop fooling around with the girls I cheated on my wife with, girls I met in bars with free-buffet happy hours and really stupid names like Thursday's or Friday's, there is no need for you to assume even a whisper of blame. My wife finally left me because of my own self-centeredness, my own neglect of her, I took the safe, and dead-end, job in the state offices because of my own indolence. How I have *wanted* to tell you this, but I have *always* been too proud. Too stubborn. But now it is too late. Listen to me.' I think I almost shouted, as he slept on and I told him once more: 'I have always loved you more than my own flesh itself. My hand before me, my very nose.' I kissed him on the cheek again. He was extremely hot in his rough slumber. But if nothing else, I assured myself, I had given it my best for once. I had accomplished this, letting go with what you might call

The Sleep Shot. And the way that nurse, the grouch Sullivan, stomped in at two minutes till eight to finally toss me out, I knew that I had, well, scored. I had sent it past the sprawled, confused goalie, over the red stripe and deep into the gulping net, ready to raise my stick in triumph to skate a victory lap around the rink at last. I had said what couldn't be said, what never had been said. And in some cockeyed, whacky, altogether-bonkers way, I knew I had connected, and I knew my father *knew*. Suddenly I could breathe easy for once, go on with my life, admitting that I soon would have to face the hard truth that my father wouldn't be with me anymore. I think Sullivan knew it too. She was visibly irked by my success. When she came in Room 317 at two minutes till eight, she was particularly gruff in picking up the magazines and newspapers I had left next to the easy chair, then gruff in tucking in the flimsy blanket around my father's gnarled toes with such precision that you could probably have checked the lines of her folds with a draftsman's steel rule when she was done. She told me it was eight, but I didn't care. I left the hospital, I went to a restaurant near my own apartment complex that night. I enjoyed a grilled blade-steak dinner, eating with a gusto I hadn't shown in years. I slept like the legendary Giant Sequoia Log later on. My father did make it through that stay in the hospital. He was brought home, survived another three months. During which time I put in a lot of hours with him, but I still never managed to tell him—him awake—the things that had to be told. But I had had my moment (time, again) in executing what might have been The Sleep Shot. And that was better than nothing."

There follows more conversation on the tape between the two of us as to whether I had the microphone of the troublesome little Panasonic recorder positioned correctly. I have not transcribed that, and for our purposes here the transcript ends at this point.

My nearly three hundred hours of conversations examine thirty-eight different "players" concerning their experience with The Sleep Shot.

IV

I would now like to provide further commentary on the observation that The Sleep Shot was repeatedly referred to with the conditional. (Footnote 9.) I do not believe that this in itself should prejudice serious scholarly attention being given to the move. I suspect that possibly because the topic has been neglected on all levels for

such an unconscionable duration that such neglect
might provide the primary reason that it is often spoken
of (if alluded to at all) tentatively and without the declar-
ative conviction ultimately reserved for The Forehand,
The Snap, or The Slap. For instance, a sixteen-year-old
subject, female, who sat for a taping spoke of it in much
the same manner. This occurred when she told of aban-
doning her six-month-old illegitimate daughter on the
steps of a rectory of a Greek Orthodox church in the
town where she had been relocated in a "home" by a
right-to-life organization. (In keeping with my policy,
lips are zipped here, and the geographic specifics will
once more be withheld.) She says, "You know, I looked at
her, this little baby in this pink quilted bunting that I
had bought just that afternoon at the Target store, you
know, and I knew then that it would be easy, you know,
as easy as one of those corny gags you pulled as a little
kid, buzzing a doorbell and then running away like all
hell, because you've got to believe me it wasn't really
cold and it had been kind of warm even for late October,
and if I didn't see somebody come to the door as I got
out of there and hid for a few minutes to watch what
would happen, I wouldn't have left her there, where she
was sleeping, so pretty, my little baby, and it was then,
right then, you know, that I let go with what my brother

the hockey player might call The Sleep Shot, or something like that, telling my baby loud that I was too
scared to keep on being a mother right then, I wasn't old
enough, and I couldn't take any more having to go to
the high school in that town either and listening to all the
boys make jokes about me in the cafeteria, their thinking
I was nasty and the way they wanted to think that I was,
and they dared each other sometimes to go right up to
me at my table and ask me if I might be able to give
them a quickie behind the second-floor lockers after last
period, things like that, you know, and I told my baby
on those steps, I talked aloud to her while she kept
sleeping and I told her that she was a good baby, not
crying very much ever since she was born, and I loved
her, really loved her, but I had to leave and it would be
better for her if she had a real family found for her by
those priests there, who at least looked so nice, and
kind, you know, their long shredded-wheat beards and
their beautiful gold hats, nothing like the yelling
preacher in the Pentecostal church in my own town
that I used to go to with my mom, where I grew up,
you know."

In each of the twelve instances that she refers to The
Sleep Shot in the complete transcript, she does it condi-
tionally, prefacing it with some variation of the phrasing

already presented, "What my brother the hockey player might call The Sleep Shot." (The occurrence of the conditional is strikingly evident in all of the transcripts, in fact, save one.)

Consider the case of a seventy-four-year-old sister who lived with her seventy-six-year-old sister. The pair of them were lifelong spinsters. She argued the entire day with the other woman, and the two of them had been going at it for the entire forty-three years that they had shared the middle deck of a three-decker in a midsize New England city, which wasn't Worcester, but maybe was quite *like* Worcester. Her transcript recounts how the arguing commenced at breakfast, over whether the orange juice was or was not fresh, or some similar petty issue; and it continued on through lunch and dinner; it reached its veritable noisy crescendo in the evening, when they abandoned their hour or so of crossword puzzles or knitting, to sit down together in the small living room for their regular couple of hours of nightly television. It would build with the bickering about which station to watch, before there came the full-fledged taunts and accusations: about the physical ugliness each charged the other with, how no man in "a thousand years" would have married the other, anyway, and the other had always been what she would always be—a pathetic spinster. The seventy-four-year-old sister tells how she would wait, later on, until she knew that her sister was sleeping deeply in her bedroom on certain evenings. She would quietly go down the hallway in the darkness, to stand in the doorway of her sister's room as the other woman continued sleeping: "It was like something that we would see on that hockey that we both hated, but that we watched on television. Or that we would make each other watch, sit through. Hockey on television was a program that we did hate so much that it was easy to take satisfaction in having the other one have to be miserable in looking at it. The hockey as mutual punishment would come after I maybe argued that we should watch the movie of the week, and then she would argue that she wanted to see something on one of those weeknight news shows, what are all just imitations of *60 Minutes,* anyway. Yes, it was almost as if I got the idea from the hockey that went on and on, until we switched to the eleven-o'clock local news, with the weather that was important, and it was what a hockey announcer might call The Sleep Shot. I just stood in that dim doorway, and I watched her dozing. I told her, then and only then, that I didn't know what would have become of me in life if I hadn't had her with me. I told her I had promised our dear mother right before she died that I would always take care of her, my sister, look after her, and now here it was, for all of our forty-three years together in the house, my sister was the one who I really needed, who took care of me, my dearest." Interestingly, in this case when I taped this elderly subject's sister speaking, that seventy-six-year-old woman's account was virtually a mirror image of what the seventy-four-year-old woman had narrated. The seventy-six-year-old sister enumerates the details of the same drawn-out bouts of daily arguing, the verbal insults and the cruelties upon cruelties that each almost vied to outdo the other with, especially in bleak winter when they often found themselves close to snowbound in the tenement. Until, come the nighttime every once in a while, the seventy-six-year-old sister would perform the identical action, waiting until she was certain that the other was asleep. She stood in the doorway of her sister's bedroom in the dark, and she uttered aloud the truth of her own feelings to the woman slumbering ten feet away from her, in bed and under "a mile-high pile of afghans and quilts," she noted. Speaking, she confessed her own real concern for the other, her love, no matter how much they argued, confessed too that she had also promised the mother years earlier that she would take care of the sister, while she herself in time came to the realization it was the caring for her by her sister that she needed the most in life, what she treasured the most.

In her narration the conditional is again used whenever it comes to any direct reference to the maneuver: "It could have been right out of that boring hockey that we usually ended up watching just to spite. My question is why do they even bother to put that junk on TV, even the cable station? Who cares? What's the point? Who can even see that little thing they keep hitting around like a bunch of crazy ants with a crumb, that puck? The announcer keeps talking about the slap shot, and I guess that's where I got it, because what I used in the dark might be called The Sleep Shot."

To emphasize once more: the repeated employment of the conditional should not be construed as detracting from the larger significance of The Sleep Shot, and remember that relying on the conditional or not, the middle-aged man who told of the visit to his father in the hospital made reference to The Sleep Shot with what can only be seen as utter conviction, complete belief.[10, 11, 12] Concrete evidence enough for shrewd Dr. Holmes himself, I would hazard to assert.

---

10. I must confess that that subject's narrative moved me most powerfully. I know that a scholar should maintain his objectivity, shouldn't turn to visceral response, but it maybe stems from the profuse mention in his transcript of the tick-tock-ticking of time itself. My wife, Clara, tries to soothe me when I tell her this. She says that mine is the to-be-expected anxiety of the scholar

V

In conclusion, no, The Sleep Shot may never join the ranks of the acknowledged staples of shooting, that Ancient Triumvirate. Yet, as I originally suggested, shouldn't we at least include it in our instruction manuals, set out, as well, to examine it with strict scientific rule to determine its dynamics (velocity, molecular composition, etc.) according to the latest rigors of laboratory study, as we have already done with The Forehand (or Wrist Shot), The Snap, and The Slap, even, occasionally, with The Flip Shot? This paper certainly cannot commence to perform any more than the spadework for the

growing older and wondering if in the *studying* that maybe the bulk of the *living* has passed one by. I tell her that a paper like this is possibly my own attempt at The Sleep Shot, these words delivered with love, to you, Proverbial Dear Reader. (Dear Sleeper? Dear Dreamer, waiting to see where the syllables will lead you next in your own somnambulistic imaginings, your picturing what the words conjure?) Actually, Clara says that I shouldn't worry about this confession. She says that there is slight chance of anybody slogging all the way through these fine-print footnotes, to make it this far to the distant No. 10 and hear me admit this. As always, Clara is right, and one of my own students here in Potsdam, a backup netminder who hopes to start for the Golden Knights next season, puts it this way: "Doc Laughton, why would anybody want to ruin his peepers reading any of them little things? Doc, what chance would you have of seeing a puck speeding at you after looking at them all afternoon? Huh?" (!!!)

11. But sometimes I feel so lonely. Sometimes I look around me on the street, even in a supermarket, and I see only loneliness and lonely people. I have cried.

12. Today Clara told me that she *is* starting to worry about me.

enormous task that awaits us. But if I have, if nothing else, raised the question of the need for additional consideration (how it would warm the chill in this aging professor's bones to see a Sleep Shot Discussion Section added to the already announced agenda for the conference at Michigan Tech next spring, April 28-30), then my purpose has been heartily served.

THE INJURY

. . . because I used to dream of rinks, and still to this day if you asked me to describe them they were the stuff of dreams, and there was a rink when I was a kid in Bantam League that they used to drive us twenty miles to for practice in the dark of night because the compressor was broken again in our mill city far north in the woods of Rhode Island, and all that I remember is the smell of refrigeration at that rink somewhere near the Providence shipyards, and the drunken attendant so old he should have been dead let us put heavy metal albums on the P.A. as we went through our starting-and-stopping drills, the intrasquad scrimmage, and there was after that the rink on the campus of the Catholic boys school in the mill city, and how could it be anything but a dream to walk into that lobby at seven o'clock on game night, early, and there was snow outside on the cozy hills, there were stars blinking, and inside in the lobby the cinderblocks were painted in the tricolor of the Montreal Canadiens themselves, glossy red, blue, and white, there were the famous teams from years gone by in framed photographs (ones with the truly legendary black hockey player from the forties, though no photographs at all from back in the sixties when the school abandoned varsity hockey completely for a while, could you believe it), there was the smell of cocoa and hot dogs for the fans, and the newspaper reporters from Providence and even Boston hanging around already trying to interview me, and they wanted to know if I knew anything about the scout from the New Jersey Devils there that night, did I know anything about the scout from the St. Louis Blues, and that was all a dream indeed, and back at the frame rowhouse later, where my grandparents had raised me, I might lie in bed in the dark and watch a snowplow with its revolving red roof beacon make another swing down the street, clanking chains, its giant blade nicking the road underneath the white in a wonderful shower of blue sparks, knowing that everything was ahead of me, that if I had scored three times with three assists that night I could probably double it if I really tried, and there was something about that girl in the bar I met the night before the injury, which of course wouldn't be for a few more years, but I did sense it when I walked into the rink in the city that night or any of those starlit winter nights back then, it was probably there when I just stared at the greenboards as the brothers in their cheap suits (no cassocks anymore) and big gold crosses looped around their necks, as they chalked away with more Algebra or more Spanish or more World History in the crack-walled classrooms, was there something then, because I was never a student, really, and if there was any consolation it was that I was a student at least when compared to the ringers who the school had been importing for most of its history from farms up in the Province of Quebec and who could go through that charade of classes pretty well themselves during the week, even if their English was barely functional and what they had of it only acquired from watching endless reruns of *CHiPs* or *The Rockford Files* on TV, but come Saturday and game night then it was all different, and they had the chance to prove themselves again on the ghostly white ice, skate blades hissing, the slap of a banana-curve stick against the hard black puck in a rifle shot, yes, compared to them and their making the school the kind of place it was, chiefly known for ruling the state schoolboy league for years back in the old days and more than ruling it lately, I *was* a scholar, and I used to laugh to see those kids from other teams get into a tangle with one of our big defensive oafs like Fleury or Cloutier in the corner, skates madly chopping away along the boards for possession of the puck, and I used to laugh indeed to see some suburban kid back off outright scared, as if he had been lured into some primal den of horror, the kind of thing his parents warned him about, where the goalie in his mask was suddenly frightening, and Cloutier or Fleury grumbled meanly in his throaty joual, the everyday blasphemous cursing of "Tabarnac!" and the rest of it, so I knew I wasn't genuinely dumb, but with a classroom record as lackluster as mine I didn't need to make any excuses why I signed pro right after I graduated from high school, why I didn't have to go through the motions of visiting college campuses with their usual walkways of brick laid like herringbone and the usual kids in turtlenecks and loafers who in fact had nothing to do with my life, because my life was hockey, and there was that girl, but that, again, would be later, and though the St. Louis organization wasn't the one I would have chosen, it was the NHL, and there was the money to sign, and with my grandfather having worked his whole life in the automotive touch-up-paint factory that had located in one of the giant red-brick textile mills—they had been divided up for "space" as the textile industry fled

the unions and started moving south even before his
time—with him having given me so much in raising
me, plus my grandmother with her take-home sewing
and her baked pies and her yellowing palm fronds from
the Easter before fanning out from the religious calen-
dar from the local funeral home always hanging there
in the kitchen—in the hot summers of mown grass and
warbly birdsong, in the cold, furnace-clanking winters
of more snow and more hockey—at last I had something to offer them, besides my grandfather's collection
of clips about me from the newspapers, even the note
in *Sports Illustrated* and, more importantly, the one in
the tabloid *Hockey News* when I signed, and what they
told me, the management, was that they wanted me
to get a little bigger, they wanted me to get used to
three games a week rather than one or two, and all of
that made sense to me, if it hadn't been for them sending me to the so-called affiliate team in that city in
Oklahoma, where the first year I worked hard and led
their team in scoring, ranked second in the entire league
in scoring, and where the second year I was already
starting to get anxious, because I wasn't eighteen anymore, and I was twenty, and at that point people did
know about me in the NHL, and everybody I ran into
who listened to the televised games there in St. Louis

told me that the color-commentary man from the two-
man announcing team for that TV coverage couldn't
help but talk about me whenever the club was losing a
game, how the franchise's future might not look bright
at the moment, but with a stickhandler like me in the
system there was real hope, and even when the club
was winning a game, he would say how if they could
edge Boston or either of the then-powerful New York
teams with the assortment they currently had at St.
Louis, imagine what they could do when a left wing
like me was finally brought up, the Stanley Cup, anything, and Mr. Shaughnessy from the front office was
frank, and once he came to the city in Oklahoma and
he took me to dinner in the restaurant of the best hotel
there, a new place of poured concrete, hanging vegeta-
tion inside like maybe the Hanging Gardens of Babylon
themselves (one of the few things, probably, I remembered from World History), completely exposed glass
elevators gliding like slow yo-yos in the enormous central lobby, a man with a tan that he had certainly
acquired from being somewhere else other than St.
Louis in the winter, Mr. Shaughnessy told me that it
was just a matter of waiting for the right moment,
there was publicity to think about, coverage, because
he assured me that a player like me didn't come along

every day, and leaning toward me he did seem to mean it in his measured syllables, confident tone, and if the dusty orange hills outside that city seemed to have nothing to do with my life right then, if the men who walked the streets there in cowboy hats and turquoise jewelry didn't either, his assurances were enough, and if St. Louis did make the play-offs, which was possible, that would be the best time to make a move, to let everybody know with fanfare what a prize the organization had found in me, though I soon knew I would have to wait another year, as March became April and the season was winding down and St. Louis had slipped in the standings, until there was a meaningless game for us coming up that evening, and rather than hang around the cheap hotel—certainly not the one where Mr. Shaughnessy and I had dined—there in the city, MacLean, Wolff, and I decided to go over to a bar for our meal with the daily living allowance we were given, a steak place called Wylie's, and there were some girls who knew who we were, and MacLean and Wolff left after a while, and the other girls left too, except for the one who stayed to talk to me and who promised she would give me a lift in her sputtering Dodge Omni if I was willing to ride in it, drive me to the Arena in plenty of time for warm-ups before the game at eight, and she was frank in telling me that she danced at a topless club, a short girl with oversize brown eyes and an almost shy way her pale pink lips wrinkled when she smiled some, she had loose auburn hair, and I suspect she didn't have to explain to me that the dancing at the club was only to pay her bills, and she hadn't lived at home since she was sixteen, and she was wearing blue jeans and a tan halter top and the kind of ridiculous cork-soled platform heels that I hadn't seen in a long time, and she told me that she was taking art classes at the local branch of the state university there in the city, and she talked of how she could easily forget those "things" her uncle did to her when she was a child back in her town not far from the Texas border, because that and the dancing and the tough club owner she was cur- rently dating seriously (proprietor of the place where she danced), none of that mattered as long as she could paint in her classes and take out of the library there more of the huge fine-arts books and look at the paint- ings, and she talked of the paintings and the painters, maybe Spanish or maybe French or maybe Italian, and it wasn't as if she was coming on to me, because she did have that boyfriend, after all, and it was as simple as the two of us killing an hour or so together before she would do something as simple as give me a lift to

the rink in the rattling Dodge Omni, she had giant
brown eyes, and I don't think I would have thought of
her again, and I don't know if I did think of her again
for a long while, but the thing is that when I look back
on it all and when I remember that night I do think of
the two of us talking together like that, I see the can-
dles in red jars covered with white mesh on the tables
in that steak place, and our team was playing the team
from Omaha, and it was one of those games so late in
the season in a minor league that you almost didn't
notice it happening, and there was a scattering of fans
in the rickety bleacher seats, the thumping drum that
one of them had brought to the games lately, a big
tom-tom, the sweetish smell of that refrigeration, the
play itself that was only a blur of their purple-and-gold
uniforms and our red-and-black ones, and it was as
routine as it being ten minutes or so into the second
period, and in a rather lackadaisical tangle for the missed
pass a two-hundred-pounder—I later learned his name
was Hennigan—from that other team simply stumbled
over his own skates to simply fly into the air and to
simply come down butt-first, his left Bauer blade just
happening to hit at the back of my own right skate and
slice through the leather to the tendon and the bone as
smoothly as a new razor blade through a bar of com-

mon bath soap, and I somehow knew already that it
was all over for me, I somehow knew that none of the
complicated operations and the long stays in the ether-
stinking hospitals that the St. Louis franchise paid for
would ever make any of it quite right, the noticeable
limp later, when I would be lucky if I could find a job
in the auto touch-up-paint place where my grandfather
still worked, punching in his card in the morning and
punching it out at night, though I did get a job there,
and sometimes now I look up from the canisters coming by on the conveyor belt to think that maybe it did
have something to do with that girl, who loved those
great artists from those faraway places in those long-
ago days, and she had to shake her breasts in front of
men every night for green bills worn as soft as flannel,
but what could it have to do with her, though it probably had everything to do with her, because I remember
her *more* than anything else, while at other times the
important thing is something else altogether, and it
wasn't that I got scared as soon as I started to talk to
her, it was more like I got scared something was wrong
long, long before that, maybe when I skated in one of
those dreamt rinks as a kid, because they surely were
dreamt, sweetly so, and now I remember, yes, it was
maybe at that rink near the shipyard in Providence

when I was a Bantam Leaguer, where we thirteen-year-olds huffingly practiced on a weekday night now and then, and we brought our Twisted Sister and Kiss albums for the attendant to put on the P.A., and when we were finished and got into minivans outside I got scared to hear a ship's horn moaning in that swallowing blue darkness (maybe *if* I hadn't been assigned to Oklahoma, maybe *if* that oaf hadn't just happened to trip over his own feet, maybe *if* I had been three rather than two yards away from him on that very ghostly white ice, or a yard the other way), and I knew then as a kid after that Bantam League practice that something wasn't right (I tell myself the tendon *wasn't* sliced beyond repair, I tell myself St. Louis *will* bring me up with fanfare, after all, next season), because sometimes when I am alone I think to myself that . . .

HOCKEY

The clubhouse of the Winter Club in Lake Forest is American Tudor with at least a half-dozen gables. The shingled sides are green and the crisscrossing beams were probably once bright buff. But the buff has turned to tan under a coating of the thick soot that blows down from the factories in Waukegan. This particular Saturday morning in 1972, fat flakes fluttered like moths and every once in a while the sun appeared in between moving clouds. Chicago lawyer John Fontaine—he had been starting right defenseman for the Harvard team in 1957 and 1958—slammed the black lid of the battered white Volvo wagon. He wore his shin pads underneath the sweatpants. He had bound them tight with hospital tape in the living room while his wife said what she always said:

"I don't know why you put yourself through it. I'm only going to have to listen to you moan about your knees for the rest of the weekend." She kissed him on the top of the head. "You're like a kid."

His stick was a stock Northland "Pro" with a five lie for a right-hander. It was new and one of the four he had bought from the remaining supply in the sports shop on LaSalle Street. The salesman told him that Northland had discontinued the straight blade in its top "Pro" line and the company now turned out only banana curves. They had come into fashion long after John had stopped playing regularly.

The ruddy-faced German attendant, Max, was behind the equipment counter at the club, smiling his usual toothy grin. The dressing room was a long corridor with benches, and framed photographs of old curling teams formed a string like boxcars along each glossily painted wall. Some of the brown-and-white group shots dated back to the twenties and before. The men in heavy coats wore matching tams for the poses and had lined up in front of the same clubhouse. The white script below listed the squad and year of each: "LFWC 1922," "LFWC 1923." Dozens of them.

At the far end of the bench, Ed Ridley laced on his scuffed skates. He seemed to sew the brass tips of the broad, dirty laces through the holes. Half finished, he stretched out one leg and with a grimace he tugged on the two taut strands, as if yanking the reins on a runaway horse. He was only a year or so older than John, but without his hair he looked maybe ten years older. He wore an old Brown University uniform jersey made of wool. The chocolate color had faded and the red stripes at the biceps were sewn-on satin and equally dull. Big moth holes splattered the back. They stretched even bigger as he leaned his overweight body down to continue lacing. John dropped his canvas bag and sat down beside him.

"I keep telling you," John said, "that sweater dates you, Ed. You're as bad as I am with my antique Northlands. I think I've bought out the last of the straight blades in Midwestern captivity. I can't get used to the curves."

Ed didn't seem interested in such talk about equipment.

"He's here," was all he said.

John probed in the bag for his skates. The room smelled of burning and a wood fire glowed like neon behind the door of a cast-iron stove. John knew who Ed meant. In fact, Ed had called him twice that week at his office to pour it all out. John found such confidence embarrassing. He didn't know Ed very well, but, of course, Ed always regarded him as a close friend because they both had played Eastern hockey. At first John feigned ignorance.

"Who's here?"

"That little bastard Lohmayer," Ed said, "that's who. He was just helloing me like I was his long-lost rich uncle."

"Look, Ed, don't jump to any conclusions. I told you that he might have been over there just for a visit. Or to do a chore."

"A chore, that's a laugh. A chore, my ass." Ed tugged again with all his strength. "They were smoking damn marijuana too. I know. Probably going at it the whole afternoon in the bedroom while they were doped. Every time I ask her about it she gives me a different story."

"Well, I hate to parcel out such obvious legal advice, but you know you have only circumstantial evidence."

"My ass. A man can tell. You know that as well as I do. You don't live with a woman for twelve years and not be able to tell. The fruit. I'll fix him today. I'll make my point."

John didn't press the issue and, in truth, he thought that maybe Ed's suspicions were justified. Ed's wife, Delia, must have been a strikingly attractive girl when younger, or, more exactly, before her face started puffing from the alcohol. Nevertheless, her lips were full, her hair a fine natural auburn, and her figure almost slight and certainly slimmer than that of most women her age, probably because she had never borne children.

It was at a small dinner get-together that fall that she
had gone as far as handling John's knee. She reached
under the table cluttered with stylish Swedish dinner-
ware and smiled. John knew he was singularly naive
when it came to such goings-on. He had married his
wife, Ruth, while still in college, and that was well
before what was eventually to be billed as the Sexual
Revolution. Ed was a bond trader for Goldman, Sachs
in Chicago. Whenever he was with John at a party,
he knitted his eyebrows as if he was thinking very
hard and said what John had heard before. "I still can
almost picture you from that time we played Harvard
in fifty-eight. It was the away game for us, all right, in
Cambridge. I remember that. Damn, if it wasn't always
the coldest rink I've ever skated in. I never loosened
up there until five minutes before the final siren. And
you had that Swede. The one who was ECAC scoring
leader through the first half of every year, before he
always folded."

"Lars. Lars Bjornson," John said.

"That's the one. What a square-headed oaf he was."

Later at the specific get-together the fall before,
Delia cornered John in the hallway. John was phoning
to tell the baby-sitter that he and Ruth were on their
way and that the car she would see coming into the

driveway in ten minutes would be theirs. Delia teetered and was very drunk. She pushed herself against his thigh and fingered the hair around his collar.

"You know, John," she said, slurring, "you Harvard man, I just want to go to party after party after party. Always. Is there anything wrong with that?"

"Of course not." What else could John say? "Nothing at all, I suppose."

"That's what I say, nothing at all."

Now John pulled his knit toque down over his ears and, with skates on, awkwardly clomped onto the planks outside. He held his stick like a shepherd's crook. The open rink was in back of the clubhouse and the diesel engine that ran the refrigeration compressor hummed lowly in a steady snore. About a dozen of the players in the makeshift Saturday-morning league were already warming up. In long, smooth strides from the hip, they skated around the oval of ice. Occasionally one would cut in to either blue line and wait for a puck, to take a practice slap. The blades swooshed and swooshed. The hard black disks exploded against the flat of the boards, rattled around the curves behind the nets. The various uniforms ranged from John's own practical sweat suit to a wide assortment of team out-fits. Some of the younger high-school kids sported imi-

tation professional jerseys. Of those, at least three had
on black Bruins uniform sweaters with the big, yellow-
edged "B" in a spoked hub on the chest. Mr. Keane
was definitely the oldest skater. He wore a ski parka
and a peaked wool lumberman's cap. Lonnie Lohmayer
wore his red Lake Forest College game jersey.
Lohmayer's father was an important Midwestern banker
who had left his vice-presidency of a leading institution
in Chicago when the Republicans took over the state-
house. He was now the head of the state's Department
of Conservation, while the newspapers speculated that
he soon might leave that post to go to Washington as
an Assistant Secretary of the Treasury. The family were
moneyed Chicagoans of long standing. When Ed had
first seen Lonnie play a couple of years before, he had
been genuinely excited.

"A natural. A goddamn natural. Maybe even put
him on defense like Orr and give him some room to
build up speed, and, believe me, with moves like that
there's no stopping the kid. We could use him at
Brown. A natural. And who says the Canucks still turn
out the best." Ed called Providence and arranged for
the coach to contact Lonnie in Lake Forest. Lonnie did
fly there for an interview and tour of the athletic facili-
ties, and was admitted. But he chose to stay near home

and go to Lake Forest College. Ed scolded him when he heard the decision. "Don't be stupid, Lon. Hockey in the East is still the only hockey. And there's always that something about the Ivy League itself. It's tough to explain. But it's something you'll have with you all your life. You don't know how many times I've heard other businessmen talk of me as an Ivy Leaguer. Ask John here who went to Harvard. Aren't I right, John? No, Lon, don't pass up a chance for the Ivy League." John remembered him saying just that.

Snow dusted the ice. Everybody agreed to cut short the warm-ups and start play quickly. The weather was obviously worsening and they wouldn't get in the usual two-hour session. The high-powered spotlights on top of the splintery poles around the rink came on and Max yelled from the clubhouse, "Is zat better?"

They simply divided into the two teams they had formed the first Saturday morning they had played, about a month before. The goalies in their rolled leather leg pads pulled down the masks that made them look tribal. They were of markedly different abilities. Coy Stout had played professionally in a West Coast league for a couple of years and had also been on one of those Clarkson College teams in the midsixties that had been so strong. John didn't know the other goalie, a high-schooler. The kid was rubbing one leg pad against the cage's red pipe like a dog trying to get rid of a tick, as he checked it was secure.

"Why don't you give us Coy this week," Ed called to the other team. "I mean, seeing we lost last week."

Nobody complained. The high-schooler lifted his stick as wide as a plank onto his shoulder and started toward the other end. Then there was a mass action of pulling jerseys over heads until one team, John and Ed's, seemed to have mostly dark and the other mostly light. In front of John, curly-haired Lonnie held out the Lake Forest shirt and was shivering a bit. He waited for John to peel off his sweatshirt. It had shrunk from repeated washing and the job wasn't entirely easy. Lonnie's bare arms were more downy than hairy and looked almost womanish. He wore only a T-shirt under the white shoulder pads trimmed with leather to keep the hard plastic from digging in.

"You should wear more than that, Lonnie," John said, "another sweater."

"Not with my speed, Mr. Fontaine." He laughed good-naturedly. He was jokingly cocky and it wasn't offensive. John found it electric, youthful. "I keep going. Don't get time to get cold." Simultaneously they aimed their heads through the necks of the exchanged shirts. "I suppose that's a comedown for you after Harvard, Mr. Fontaine." Lonnie laughed again.

The first time:

Lonnie pumped full speed, holding his stick out in front of him plow style and pushing the puck on the taped flat of it. He wasn't dribbling, because dribbling only slows you down on such breakaways. John watched him from behind the bolted door of the players' compartment. He was surprised that Ed even caught up with the boy—he was so fast. Ed didn't go for the puck. He just threw Lonnie into the direction he was speeding, the way a football linebacker might shove a receiver out of bounds. Actually, it was a clean, legal check. Lonnie hit hard against the boards and the crushing sound brought loud cheers of approval so early in the game.

"All-ri-ight!"

"How you hit, big Ed-dee!"

The flakes were smaller now, but more steady. They were like white gauze in front of the light of the powerful lamps that looked purple in intensity. John himself played a cautious game and he knew he had to be careful of his troublesome knees. In his senior year of college the cartilage had strangely given out. Another operation might leave him with a limp. He usually played on defense with Mr. Keane, who was over fifty.

Together, they liked to pass back and forth on the blue line. They would work methodically to confuse completely the organization of the other side, before they fed the puck to the moving forwards, hopefully for a score. The game couldn't last much longer. When John got the puck on his stick, he strained just to keep sight of it. The snow was almost as deep as the blade. Once, he flipped a pass to Mr. Keane and the dragging disk lost momentum at midice. It was left there for galloping Lonnie to pick up. He zigzagged a few strides and then slipped a soft backhand shot to the goal's upper corner, where it hit the netting, a strong hand trying to punch through it. Coy Stout lay sprawled on his stomach. He got up to his knees, pushed the mask back on his sweating face, and laughed, "Nice shot, Lonnie."

John hated watching Ed rough up Lonnie in the congestion that developed in front of the cages. Ed incessantly elbowed the kid's ribs. In the middle of one battering, Lonnie simply forgot about the play and said, "This is ridiculous." He skated to the bench and told somebody else to take his turn on the line.

The second time:

Lonnie must have seen Ed coming. The kid was scrapping with his skate for a loose puck at the boards. Ed charged to flatten him and Lonnie dodged. Without

Lonnie's body for a cushion, Ed absorbed the full impact of his own sprint, and his bald head banged hard into the galvanized hexagon-loop wire above the boards. No doubt he was hurt. Most everybody skated onto the ice and Mr. Keane said they should stand back and give him some air. Ed slowly put his gloved hand to the right eye. Red trickled from the bushy brow and he tugged off his glove to feel the cut. Ed loped back to the bench and Mr. Keane told him he best "Call it a day." Ed didn't listen. John sat down beside him. Grinding his yellowed teeth, Ed said, "I'll kill the bastard now. I'll kill him."

John hoped nobody else heard such foolish talk. Coy Stout suggested they abandon the game altogether and one of the high-schoolers, more exuberant, offered the usual, "Next goal wins it." They never kept track of the exact numerical score, but they always seemed to know who won by the feeling that one team had had an easier time of it.

"Damn this," said Ed. "I've always been an easy bleeder. Something about my skin." He scooped some snow off the bench and held it to his head. Its white darkened. "Damn."

"It will be a lot safer," John said, "when they get the new Plexiglas. That wire is damn dangerous. You know, maybe you should get a tetanus shot."

But Ed wasn't listening. He was staring at the game. Across the action of slamming sticks, reddened faces, and pleading shouts for a pass and being in the clear, John could see his wife, Ruth, with their two children. Ruth wore an old camel's-hair coat with the collar upturned. Her hair looked very dark and her skin very clear in the cold. Admittedly, she had become heavier in the last few years. But John, sitting there, thought how handsome she always was in winter. He thought that she had watched him play hockey so often. *Hockey*.

On the ice again, John exchanged passes with Mr. Keane. Ed had missed his turn on defense and now played on wing. John noticed Ed waiting with his stick upraised to signal he was indeed in the clear. John lobbed the puck to him in the air, so it wouldn't drag in the snow on the ice.

"Take it!" somebody yelled.

"All yours, Ed!" somebody else echoed.

John watched and felt a long pang in his stomach. Lonnie, obviously scared, was no more than ten feet in front of Ed, facing him. Lonnie kept his knees close together and his stick blade on the ice, like a goalie, for the block. Ed cocked his own stick up behind him to his shoulder as he readied for the hard slap. He grinned and the blood on his face was running again in a squiggle. It probably lasted only an instant, but to John it seemed forever. He remembered all the injury he had seen in his many years of hockey. A puck to the head *could* kill a man. He remembered noses looking like dough thrown against a breadboard. Teeth hanging from shreds of ragged gum or being spit out like a mess of half-chewed peppermint Lifesavers. He hated to think of the eyes. Above all, he hated to think of a squashed lid immediately starting to swell like a veiny rotten plum. Yes, it seemed forever.

John wanted to save Lonnie with a lunging tackle of Ed. He had to stop Ed or at least shout for Lonnie to protect himself—to duck! But he didn't. Ed grimaced and let go.

Lonnie never flinched. He didn't have to. When Ed's shot finally came, it was a weak, heartless dribbler. John would never know if Ed intended such or simply hit the wrong way, like a nervous golfer. The puck was a wheel as it rolled with a wobble through the snow. Ed appeared blank, lost in the action, and already was leaving. Mr. Keane tipped the puck past Coy Stout and the goalie surely let him make the score. Play ended for another Saturday. Ed shook his head. He was the first one off the ice and the first one into the clubhouse. The

German, Max, held open the door for him and John heard the attendant say, "A bad one, Mr. Ridley. Coming down za lake. Za radio man says all za lakes will be buried by morning."

John walked over the path of boards. His son stood there outside, waiting for him.

"Hey, Dad, where did you get that shirt? It's neat." John's son was ten. "It's almost like a Chicago Black Hawks uniform." The boy ran his mittened hand along the stripes at the waist. "Yeah, red with white stripes just like that. Even the black."

Lonnie came up to them. He had John's sweatshirt in his hand. He looked worried and was pale. He didn't joke.

"Here, Mr. Fontaine." His voice wasn't even strong.

"Oh, you didn't have to worry about me running off with your uniform, Lonnie. I'm on my way to the club-house."

"Ah, well, I'm sort of in a hurry. I think I'll just head home."

"Sure," John said.

Lonnie smiled. Ruth and John's daughter, Annie, found them there. The girl was putting a handful of snow and leaves to her mouth.

"Put that down, Annie," Ruth said.

Lonnie had on his own shirt now.

"That's almost like a Black Hawks shirt, mister," Little John said.

Lonnie managed to smile again and tramped off. He didn't go through the clubhouse, though. He headed around the side of the building where there were bare forsythia bushes, white skeletons in the snow.

"Isn't that the Lohmayer boy," Ruth said, "who your friend Ed Ridley wanted to go to Brown? Another one of Ed's famous ideas up in smoke." She never took Ed seriously.

"Yes, that's Lonnie," John said.

"He looks sick. He should have the sense to wear more than that in this cold. It's obvious he's coming down with something."

John was a little weak himself. He was drained, tired, glad it was over. *Hockey.*

It was Saturday afternoon. John felt entirely clean and fit after showering. He followed Ruth and the children through the supermarket, and the slight stiffness in his arms and shoulders from the play was almost pleasant. His knees were fine. Boots dripped and dripped on the market's muddy floor. Low refrigerators with mirrors behind them held the waxy cardboard packages of frozen foods. John watched Ruth reach in for a box of Bird's Eye Oriental Vegetables with a bright picture of fresh pea pods, onions, and mushrooms on a chopping board on the front. He stared at the reflection of the box and her slim fingers holding it in the mirror.

"Did you like these last time we had them?" she asked.

"What?" He was vacant. *Hockey.*

"These vegetables. Did you like them?"

"Yes. Of course."

The shopping cart shivered on wobbly wheels. She described clearly to the butcher exactly how she wanted him to cut the top-round roast that was on sale. The man in his blood-splattered coat appeared pleased to deal with a woman who knew exactly what she wanted. Enamored with the very fullness of his wife's behind, John felt stupid in his affection that sometimes had such adolescent fervor.

Later, John was lying down on the sagging sofa on the sunporch. He was comfortably exhausted from the morning's game by this time. The portable television's gray light was drugging. The program, a wild-animal or adventure show, was narrated by an Englishman with a broad accent, and it was a tour of a game preserve at the very tip of South Africa. The springbok had flowing horns and they grazed right on the beaches. "The beauty of this park," the Englishman said, "is the fantastic juxtaposition of these lovely wild animals and the breathtaking panorama of this beach, these cliffs, and this ocean." Little John came up to the sofa with a sheet of manila drawing paper on which he had sketched a hockey player in brisk strokes. The teachers at his elementary school down the street said he was a natural artist. He got it from his mother. John had bought him a box of artist's chalk for his birthday and the boy treasured the pastels like sticks of gold bullion. He inspected them to make sure they wore evenly and kept them meticulously arranged in the slots of the case provided. The skating figure shed a shadow on the ice. At ten he already knew about light angles and such.

"So, what's this?" asked John. He had one hand behind his head for a pillow.

"A player," his son said. "And he's wearing a red shirt like the one the man let you use today. What does 'LF' stand for?"

"Lake Forest. The college."

"Oh yeah, that's right."

A clanking plow passed outside with the chains on its tires thumping. The sound reminded John of the

New Hampshire town where he had grown up. He didn't want to think of Ed Ridley just then. He didn't want to think of Lonnie Lohmayer either. The theme song for the wild-animal show was a classical piece that John seemed to recognize. The white credits rolled up the screen.

"Is your father sleeping?" It was Ruth from the kitchen.

"I don't think so," Little John answered her.

"Well, why don't you turn off that set and let him. Come in and draw in here."

With eyes wide open, John watched the boy fiddle with the switch on the pole lamp, then he got the television set's knob in a single twist. The bright grew smaller to the size of a pinpoint. It was like a distant star and hung on for a long while. Finally, the tube was only a seal-colored bubble of reflection. The outside, where the white birches grew in clusters, was almost dark. The inside, with the light off, was even darker. John liked the winter. He liked hockey. *Hockey.*

He had grown up in the French end of the mill town. The porched, two-story house was like all the others on the street. The lawns were small and divided by driveways of twin cement tracks always sprouting weeds in the summer. Most of the fathers of the other boys worked the humming looms of the textile mills.

They were red-brick monstrosities with green-painted windows. John had thought those mills were bona fide castles till he was six. *Hockey.* His father was a school-teacher and though he never earned very much, he had a regular income. The mill workers were often laid off for months at a time. John hadn't asked his father for the hockey gloves. The man simply returned from monitoring late detention one weekday afternoon and put them on the kitchen table. They smelled of their soft leather and must have cost fifteen dollars even then. On the stiff, gauntletlike cuff, a little armadillo was neatly depicted. The caption below read, ARMOR PLATED. But John wouldn't wear them when he tramped through the woods for the afternoon choose-up games at the pond beside one of the mills. There the ice was hard and black, and they dragged fallen branches onto the surface to mark the goals. In truth, John hid the gloves in the cellar behind the plastered furnace boiler, because he hated to flaunt such opulence in front of the other boys, who were such a scruffy lot. They talked with accents left over from the French they were raised on. They wore gold miraculous medals trimmed with baby-blue ribbons—their mothers pinned them on their jackets in case they fell through. Sometimes John returned home and hit the gloves

around the basement. He dribbled them with his stick
to scuff that amber leather. If his father saw them, he
wanted to make sure the man thought they were being
put to hard play.

John always admitted that Harvard took him to
play the sport. He had gone to the high school in the
town and the year he graduated the team easily won
the state championship. Ruth was from Philadelphia
and went to Radcliffe. She had gone to a posh boarding
school in Germantown. Both her parents were professors and, besides that, they were divorced. Back then it
all seemed entirely sophisticated to John. He used to
feel like a bumpkin around her. At college she princi-
pally wanted to paint and she spent most of her four
years frustratedly complaining that Harvard offered no
real studio art courses. He knew she noticed him only
because he played hockey. She loved to show her
friends his glossy photograph in the window of Elsie's
Lunch. During the season, pictures of the starters lined
the bulletin board there. The camera had caught John
coming to a sudden stop. A surf of ice shavings blasted
like rhinestones in front of him and he had his stick
upraised. He wasn't wearing his bridge and looked
menacing indeed without the two side teeth. She once
told him that a boarding-school girlfriend had asked

her if John was a "ringer."

"A ringer?" Ruth said to her. She thought that the girl was inquiring if John intended marriage—would he give her a ring. "We haven't talked yet about what either of us will do after college."

"Don't be a dummy," the other girl said. "I mean, the name is French. Fontaine. Did they bring him from Canada to play?"

Hockey.

He closed his eyes, opened them, and closed them again.

He fell into a dream in which he heard sirens as he talked on the phone. He might have been in his office or in a downtown restaurant where the white-jacketed waiter had told him during lunch that there was a call for him. On the other end of the line, Ed Ridley said he was at his own house in Lake Forest. He babbled, and at first John didn't want to let himself believe it.

"What?" asked John.

"P-please," stammered Ed Ridley. "Oh, please, John, just tell me what the hell to do now!"

"I knew you were going to do it!"

"I didn't mean to. It just . . . it just happened and . . ."

"Are you *sure*?"

"Oh, God, *am* I sure. I've tried everything. That mouth-to-mouth stuff. It's no good. The rescue is here now, they're outside. I've shot him!"

"I knew you would. You're a fat-headed fool, Ridley! You're. . . ."

John tensed on the sofa as if something electrical had stung him. He felt his whole body jerk. He opened his eyes to see the shadows of the butterfly chairs, the pole lamp, and a contraption that his daughter had been given for Christmas the year before called "Barbie's Penthouse." He rolled to one side and then settled on his back again. He savored the heaviness of just lying there.

The next dream was deeper and maybe he was dozing for a half-hour before it came. It probably had nothing to do with hockey. Or, if it did, he would never know, because he was somewhere else that he would never remember. Here—where he had been, in this world where hockey is played—another clanking plow passed. Its chains thumped and blue sparks blinked along the steel blade nicking the road.

Van Arsdale's Pond

The boys said they didn't care if the ice wasn't good on Whittaker's Pond, because there was the other pond they had heard about. No, they had never been there, but that didn't matter—they had heard.

Maybe the ice had come suddenly in December, before Christmas the way it sometimes could, altogether unexpected. Somebody's older brother inevitably had a tale about skating on Thanksgiving Day, when the cut-out turkeys were still scotch-taped to the windows of Nausauket Elementary School, but nobody really believed that. Though by early December it might take only two or three truly cold nights of the red alcohol in the thermometer outside a frosted window cringing low in the clear, frigid darkness, and then lower. And to see Whittaker's Pond then was to come upon it the next afternoon after the last buzzing school bell had finally sounded at three, to hike the half-mile or so off the state two-lane and over the dun-colored knolls, then into the shadowy woods proper with the crunching leaves and the minty pines and the bunches of white birches, to finally spot it below, Whittaker's Pond. Before a snowfall, the ice might be glaringly black, not frozen much up by the end with the earthen dam that the Eagle Scouts had rebuilt who knows how many years before (had any kid actually *known* an Eagle Scout?), and surely more than the rule-of-thumb six inches thick down by the shallow end where the squat hoarfrosted bushes grew right through the surface and would at least give you something to grab onto if you were the first kid gingerly inching out to test if it was safe (one flimsy shoe or boot placed soft, like a floating dandelion puff, then the other). But it probably wasn't December, and the issue now was not really whether the ice was safe, but whether it was smooth enough and reasonably skatable after a midseason thaw. And, again, even if the ice wasn't good, they knew about the other pond.

One thing that was certain was that the boys' mothers, young, did what they always did on winter afternoons. They took time away from their sitting in front of a rattling Singer machine, or baking pies in the cramped kitchens heady with the aromas of shortening and cinnamon, and they got everything ready for the boys. One mother liked to place her son's long wool skating socks, the gray ones, on the radiator in the hallway; she would have them warmed when he came through the back

storm door, in such a hurry because "There's ice, Mom!"
and the others were waiting for him and he was already
late. Another mother might simply gather together what
she knew her son would need, have the scuffed skates and
the taped stick ready, the puck on which she noticed
what she had never noticed before: the boy had carved his
initials into the hard black rubber, probably with a carpenter's nail, and how lovely was his attempt at scrolling
the letters for the job that must have taken him hours,
making each period after each letter an ornate asterisk.

A moment like that could render a mother, standing
in her housewife's dress and apron, staring at the puck,
very sad.

And the boys were not in the classroom any longer.
They were not gazing at the clock above the coatroom,
and they were not banging past each other in their crazed
charge to flee through the big battered green doors and
out of the place at last. At this point they had already
been home, already enjoyed the snack of Hydrox cookies
and milk that waited for them, let's say, on a chrome-
trimmed kitchen table, and the pack of them, six all told,
were trudging up a knoll, there beside the two-lane. They
wore galoshes, heavy coats, and peaked leather caps or
knit toques. They carried their skates by putting them

onto the blade end of the stick, either slung by the loop of the tied-together dirty laces or the stick poked through the handy space below the sole on the skates' bottoms; they jutted the sticks over their shoulders, and the effect was that of what could be seen in old fairy-tale books, telling the story of any meandering tramp with his long pole and full sack of belongings toted that way, exactly the same for all of them.

One could watch them from a distance, going down the snow-covered slope of another knoll now; they were a moving line, a queue, each with the stick over the shoulder, the skates dangling. They appeared to be on a real journey, not just a long walk to a pond. They entered into the woods.

There was the sharp, clean smell of the snow itself that slapped your nostrils when you inhaled. A fat jay on a bare tree limb screeched away at them, then nearly detonated off in a swoosh of fluttering blue, the branch still shaking.

Of course, the boys talked:

"I wonder about it," a tall one for his age said, "and who knows what Whittaker's will be like after so much melting."

"You could be right." A rosy-cheeked boy said that, optimistic. "But I have a feeling it's going to be OK, and it will be good ice, I'm sure, even if we haven't had ice for a week."

"More than a week," the taller boy said.

"It warmed up over the weekend," one of the twins said.

"It did, you're right about that," the other one of the twins said. "It warmed up a lot over the weekend."

"But last night was cold, and that's all that counts," the rosy-cheeked boy told them.

"I suppose," one of the twins said.

"Yeah," the other said.

Because this wasn't like the first freeze of a season whatsoever. As already said, with a first freeze, be it the reputed Thanksgiving surprise or late ice, not coming until a week after New Year's, the situation was basically simple. First the fragile skin of a surface, then the huge extended star patterns in it when it turned solid, and finally the thick, lenslike covering, sturdier and sturdier, as hopefully the subsequent days brought nothing more in the sky than the welcome gray dimness, no sun and only cold. But once a surface had formed for the year, usually intact until March, any number of variations could occur.

If it stayed cold, there eventually came the snow, sometimes a howling blizzard, and the cover of accumulated white posed the source of the complication. In the most frigid of winters, when the weather lady on the one television station that came in clear in this part of the state sang of storms flopping down from Canada one after another, in that kind of cold the boys could shovel a rectangle for play. And while that surface could quickly be gouged to ruts from the wear of consecutive afternoons of games, and while there was always the nuisance of losing a puck into the downy dust of the pile when somebody missed a pass along the edge, that meant, nevertheless, they had ice, and ice didn't have to be perfect: nobody ever expected perfect ice after the first freeze of the year, that famous black ice. The boys sometimes talked of how they almost had it in them to rig up long plywood slabs with the stems of old broken hockey sticks for handles nailed to the boards, for the variety of ready plows that teenage guys on the high-school team heartily manned, four of them to a slab, pushing hard to clean a whole pond for practice sessions. But, understandably, these boys were too young and not that organized; just lugging a couple of heavy snow shovels through the woods and to Whittaker's Pond was work enough, a feat to challenge Hannibal with his bell-jangling elephants transporting war supplies across the towering Alps, as far as they were concerned. The real problems began with a midseason melt. The snow could turn to slush, refreezing when the next cold front arrived in uneven lumps like a cake that hadn't risen right, or, much worse, porous, crusted, and flimsy with no surface gloss to speak of, everywhere a pinto patterning of giant air bubbles each a few feet wide to be crunched into by blades, what their skates could barely stumble across, never mind glide over. In short, the boys had no idea what they would find at Whittaker's Pond after this midseason warming and the return to the cold. They could be lucky, certainly, and sometimes a melt was thorough enough to mean a flood of water atop the surface all over again, and then a fine glaze indeed with the subsequent refreezing.

They walked on through the woods. The twins bounced lines off one another like echoes, their talk never saying much of anything. The rosy-cheeked boy kept telling everybody that he knew the ice would be good, and the taller boy wasn't sure of that or much else lately, but he was willing to try to believe that all would prove OK. The group of them probably talked about the Providence Reds hockey team. They probably talked about how tough the cattle-drive master, Gil Favor, was on *Rawhide,* how funny the show with Dobie Gillis could be. They probably talked as well about the faraway territory called "girls," somebody claiming that in his classroom that very morning there was a prime example of a girl's bossiness, then playing up to the teacher, from a certain Cheryl Beaupre, a performance nobody would *believe;* then somebody else claiming that in his classroom that same afternoon he had managed to execute his old trick with the tawnily blond Diane Maloney yet another time—dropping his yellow pencil to the linoleum under his desk, pretending for a long while that he couldn't find it around the worn-shiny steel stem of that desk, and the whole time enjoying a leisurely ogle of Diane's panties, kelly green this particular day. But mostly they talked about the ice, what they might find at Whittaker's Pond. There was a measure of bullying, sad to say, from the boy who was noticeably wiry, gruff too; he picked on a boy with a soft voice who always found himself last in the queue.

"It could have melted a lot, it might not even be safe," the bullying boy said, and turning to the boy with the soft voice, he told him, "What if you fell through?"

The soft-voiced boy didn't answer him.

"You don't drown, you know, you just go into shock, like somebody plugged one of your fingers into a hungry hundred-and-twenty-volt socket. Freezing shock, worse than electric shock, and just like that."

He snapped his fingers, leered at the other boy. He was delighting in scaring him.

"Shut up," one of the twins told the bully.

"Yeah, shut up," the other one said.

At home the mothers maybe returned to the sewing

machine, or started on what had to be done at the ironing board, the electric flat fragrant of heat and scorched cotton, and one of those dime-store plastic daisies stuck into the top of a soda bottle used for sprinkling water during the task. Maybe one of them walked to a window, put fingers to the cold pane, and whispered aloud but to nobody in particular: "My son is in the woods now, going to the pond. All I can do is hope that all is well and safe for him." And the fathers? The fathers worked jobs like that of auto mechanic or assistant records clerk somewhere in the steam-heated basement of the town hall, and occasionally one of them, weary at this stage in the long afternoon, would just sigh to think, "How, oh how, did I ever get this old?"

Until, as soon as the boys could see through the trees to the lopsided oval of Whittaker's Pond, they knew that the worst thing imaginable—the ultimate destruction of midseason ice—had happened. And any good luck with the days of melt producing a sizable water coating that in turn pristinely refroze, those hopes were gone when they saw what they saw: yes, there had been snow that melted to slush, but somewhere in the process, kids, probably not even in grade school, had committed the transgression of transgressions, stomping indiscriminately and savagely on the pond with their rubber boots in a maddened patterning of indented dance steps, which had eventually frozen solid and ruined any chance of decent skating, any chance of pond hockey completely.

The bullying boy seemed to take satisfaction in this disaster, saying:

"Just as I figured, a total mess." He turned again to the boy he had been picking on, adding, "And now you won't even be able to freeze to death, or drown."

"It must have been real little kids," that other boy said blankly in reply, "kids who nobody ever told that you aren't supposed to ruin ice. They must have come from those new houses in the plat in back."

The boys stared in disbelief. (Years later the bullying boy, Jimmy Arsenault, was killed in a foreign war that nobody supported, as his valiantly attempting to save a wounded pal brought him close to an enemy sniper. The timid boy, Wayne Wright, might have gone on to a position of great success if the rule worked that the world eventually found a balance in such opposites, like the bullying boy becoming a selfless battle hero of sorts. But that didn't happen. The timid boy didn't turn out to be a known movie star, or even a mayor; he would never marry, would in time end up in a meaningless town office job himself, living alone with a tiger-striped cat in a local apartment house, where the neighbors considered him strange. Concerning what became of somebody in life, as with what kind of ice you might find, there often seemed little more than sheer chance.) Meanwhile, the twins were now starting to growl their disappointment.

"Shit," one said.

"Yeah," said the other, "shit."

(Who knew what became of them, because wasn't it true that nobody ever knew or heard what became of twins later on? It seemed that being twins in itself was a full-time justification, a defining task, in life; they were the Ericksons.)

"There's the other pond," the optimistic boy said. "The kids from over on Long Street were talking about it at school. They say it's better than Whittaker's, anyway, and with it sitting on a chicken farm like that, nobody much knows about it except for them and the farmer. Nobody will have wrecked that ice, and they're all probably out there already, those Long Street kids, they're probably playing and having a ball. Who cares about this?" He tipped his head toward the pond, Whittaker's, which all of them had been anticipating skating on since they had woken that morning, when they realized exactly how cold it had been during the night and that the thaw was finally over; they had been thinking about it the entire day in the blur of the several hours of school. "Who *cares?*"

But the twins announced they were tired. They didn't feel like tramping through the snow anymore, would just as well head home and watch late-afternoon TV cartoons in their basement rumpus room. And the bullying boy, possibly out of inherent perversity, argued that in his opinion you couldn't even get to Van Arsdale's chicken farm this way, through these woods, and the soft-voiced, bullied boy needed no more persuasion than that and completely agreed with him.

"But what about what we've been saying the whole way here," the rosy-cheeked boy said, "how we kept telling each other that if the ice is no good on Whittaker's, we can still go to the other pond, a *better* pond, I tell you."

"That was way back then," one of the twins said.

"Way back when," the other said, liking the rhyme of it, chuckling.

"That's funny," the first twin said.

"Yeah," the other said.

The entire contingent was about to abandon the plan of going on, but the boy who was tall for his age spoke up:

"I'll go with you," he said to the optimistic boy.

"Well, here's somebody who wants good ice," that boy replied to him.

The others were soon gone, and the two remaining

boys crossed the pond's ruined ice, waded slow through the deep drifts along the other side, and headed on through the pillars of the tall trees. The day was still now, losing light. They walked for a half-hour.

"I think they might have been right," was the only thing the rosy-cheeked boy said.

And with that he pivoted, and also was gone.

So, the boy who was taller kept going without the rosy-cheeked boy. (Here there was predictability: the rosy-cheeked boy, cheerful by nature, eventually attended a good college, then worked to establish his own successful real estate agency; he would have a wonderful wife and five children. His name was Alan Lelaidier.) The taller boy marched through the trees, and he wondered why he was determined to go on, to be frank. Was it to prove a point? Or did he, in fact, expect to find good ice at the pond at Van Arsdale's chicken farm, a crew of boys playing hockey there and welcoming him into their game? He didn't know. To be frank again, he wasn't as much as sure if he had *actually* gone into the woods with skates and hockey stick along with the bunch of his pals that afternoon, or if this too were but another imagining, the way so much felt to him like but another imagining lately. And in the imagining, the insubstantiality of it,

smoke wafted from chimneys in the frozen late afternoon
of a forgotten Rhode Island town, where mothers kept so
lovingly busy in warm, wooden bungalows, and fathers,
weary, wrestled through jobs that seemed to matter little, to lead nowhere. The boy was cold, and when he
got to the top of another knoll, into a clearing with some
tumbledown snow-fencing, he could see that the sky had
lifted; a band of the palest of blue was widening above
the hills black with their blanketing of winter trees, and
he could see the buttery wedge of a moon. Without the
cloud cover, the night would be very, very cold.

His toes were numb in the galoshes, he flipped the
fuzzy gray earflaps down on his peaked leather cap,
which felt good. (But was this really him? Was this Larry
Gaudette? Or was this the shadow of somebody he often
suspected he was, alone, the way he would always be
alone in the course of an early marriage that didn't work
out, then separated from his children in later years with
carpentry jobs in Connecticut and upstate New York,
places that were continents away from who he was, where
he was from—more alone than ever. He *was* almost
watching a boy trudge along.) Still, he didn't care about
the cold. He could picture the pond at Van Arsdale's. He
could envision it protected in a little bowl of hills, the
farmer's white clapboard house and the rickety red

chicken sheds on a rise beyond that, the lights in the house's windows yellow at dusk.

He saw himself skating on a beautifully glassy surface, good ice, all right, dribbling a puck, telling himself how he had never liked anything in the world, loved anything, as much as to hear his blades cutting over the ice, to be skating.

He trudged on, suspecting that possibly it—*everything, always*—could turn out OK, even if somebody like the overoptimistic boy, who had left, ultimately saw folly in it. There *might* be good ice, and trying to think only of that, he, like so many of us, continued deeper and deeper into the woods.

Coda:
Two Great Quotes

"Another thing that absolutely petrified—and enraged—me was stick-swinging. Dennis Hextall, one of the worst offenders, gave me great respect for the injury potential of wood when he nearly put the blade of his stick through my neck. Of the players still around, Dave Hutchison, Cashman, and Bobby Schmautz are the leading lumberjacks."

—Dave Schultz of the Philadelphia Flyers, in
The Hammer: Confessions of a Hockey Enforcer

"That night I woke up in a cold sweat after dreaming about having my leg cut off. I started thinking about things I take for granted, like buying a pair of pants or shoes. And that's when I went a little paranoid—nutsy. I figured, no running, no walking with groovy chicks along lonely beaches. . . ."

—Derek Sanderson of the Boston Bruins, in
I've Got to Be Me